"Why is this so awkward, Ty?"

Kate asked softly.

"I think it's because we've got this thing for each other."

"What?" Breathing out startled laughter, Kate looked down at her coffee. "You're *bad*," she said, shaking her head.

He didn't respond right away. Instead, he tore open a packet of sugar, tapped the white stream of granules into his cup and stirred the liquid slowly. "But that's what you want, isn't it?" He set down the spoon and looked at her. "A bad boy who'll muss up your hair a little, your clothes, maybe even your life?" His voice dropped lower and became slightly sandy. "Isn't that what you want?"

Kate's fingertips whitened against the cup. He read her too well. She took a sip of the coffee and found it scalding hot and strong. She also found it delicious. "Raphaell—Ty," she said, "I'm not sure we've got the timing right on this coffee date. It feels too soon, doesn't it? Maybe we should give ourselves some time."

"How much time?"

"A year or two?"

Dear Reader:

Happy holidays! All the best wishes to you for a joyful, loving holiday season with your family and friends.

And while celebrating, I hope that you think of Silhouette Romance. Our authors join me in wishing you a wonderful holiday season, and we have some treats in store for you during November and December—as well as during the exciting new year.

Experience the magic that makes the world so special for two people falling in love. Meet heroines that will make you cheer for their happiness and heroes (be they the boy next door or a handsome, mysterious stranger) that will win your heart. Silhouette Romances reflect the magic of love—sweeping you away with books that will make you laugh and cry, heartwarming, poignant stories that will move you time and time again.

During the next months, we're publishing romances by many of your all-time favorites such as Diana Palmer, Brittany Young, Lucy Gordon and Victoria Glenn. Your response to these authors and others in Silhouette Romances has served as a touchstone for us, and we're pleased to bring you more books with Silhouette's distinctive medley of charm, wit and—above all—*romance*.

I hope you enjoy this book and the many stories to come. Come home to Silhouette Romance—for always!

Sincerely,

Tara Hughes
Senior Editor
Silhouette Books

SUZANNE FORSTER

The Passions of Kate Madigan

Published by Silhouette Books New York

America's Publisher of Contemporary Romance

SILHOUETTE BOOKS
300 E. 42nd St., New York, N.Y. 10017

ISBN: 0-373-08627-X

First Silhouette Books printing January 1989

All the characters in this book are fictitious. Any
resemblance to actual persons, living or dead, is
purely coincidental.

Printed in the U.S.A.

SUZANNE FORSTER

started her writing career by accident. Literally. She took up writing while confined to bed after a car accident, and her first published book was discovered quite accidentally by an editor who read it while judging the finalists in the 1984 Romance Writers of America writing contest. Accidents do happen, but Ms. Forster's talent is the real key to her success.

ACKNOWLEDGEMENTS

Heartfelt thanks to Gini Wilson,
a friend and fellow writer,
for her support and encouragement.
She saw the potential in
The Passions of Kate Madigan
at a time when I was ready
to set the project aside.

My thanks also to the staff of the Criminal Justice Training Center at Golden West College, and especially Dan Lyons, their executive training adviser, for his advice and counsel, his patience with all my questions, and his willingness to let me observe the day-to-day workings of a police academy. Frank Patino, the assistant dean, and Chris George, a recruit training adviser (aka "Dragon Lady") were also particularly helpful and deserve special recognition. I wish to thank them all for their unstinting help—and for understanding that I had to take some "literary license" with academy procedure for the dramatic purposes of the story.

Chapter One

Sergeant Kate Madigan heard the low wolf whistle as soon as she entered the classroom. Without the slightest hitch in her steady stride, she walked to the front of the room, set her briefcase on the desk, opened it and took out the material for that night's orientation session. Wolf whistles, bawdy winks, insinuating remarks—she'd seen and heard it all in her five years as a drill instructor at Pacific Police Academy.

Silently Kate acknowledged the buzz of low voices and laughter and decided she would let these first-nighters have their fun a little longer. She had an advantage the recruits didn't have. She knew what was coming next.

She took her baton from its leather case and set it on the counter, then she began sorting course schedules and handouts into neat stacks. Finally, when the noise subsided and a waiting hush fell over the room, she brought down the briefcase lid with a quick, explosive crack.

"Did I hear somebody *whistle*?" she asked, looking up, scanning the startled faces of thirty-three male and seven female rookies.

Dead silence was her answer.

"That's what I thought." She consulted her watch. "As of now, 1800 hours, nobody in this room makes a sound without permission. Is that clear? I don't want to hear a hiccup unless it's been okayed by me first." She swept the class with her eyes, daring the recruits to challenge her.

Immediately the **sil**ence turned uneasy, expectant. Kate knew this was the crucial moment when she took control— or lost it. First nights were always a test of her ability to assert her authority, and experience had taught her if she prevailed at this point the rest of the session would be infinitely easier—for everyone concerned.

She wasn't dealing with the regular recruits. This class met evenings and weekends. It was for reserve officers, a program open to men and women ranging in age from eighteen to fifty-five. The enrollees came from every conceivable walk of life. Most of them chose this route because they held day jobs and some were motivated by the wrong reasons— carrying a firearm being one—but most of them were looking for a legitimate way to get into law enforcement either as reserve or as full-time officers. At least Kate hoped they were. She never knew quite what she was getting in a reserve class, which made everything a little dicier.

"Permission to speak, ma'am?" one of the recruits said, raising his hand.

"Your name, recruit," Kate said.

"Parker, ma'am."

"Ask your question, Parker."

"What do we do if nature calls, ma'am?" Snickers of laughter erupted around the room, and a smart-aleck grin spread across Parker's boyish face.

"Are you asking permission to go the rest room?"

"Uh...yes, ma'am?" More snickers.

"Sit in it, Parker."

As laughter broke out, Kate picked up her baton and brought it down with a sharp crack on the desk, startling them into silence. "I want it quiet in here!" she ordered. "*Dead* quiet."

She walked around the desk and stood in front of it, slapping the baton against her palm. It was her Patton imitation, and a darn good one she'd been told. "Apparently, you people didn't take me seriously," she warned. "I said not a *sound* without permission. That laughter is going to cost this entire class thirty push-ups. *Now!* Down on the floor next to your desks. Count 'em out, and give me a *ma'am* with every one."

It was chaos as the recruits scrambled onto their hands and knees, one knocking his desk over in the process.

"Hit it!" Kate ordered.

"One, *ma'am*, two, *ma'am*, three, *ma'am*," they counted out, the entire class bobbing up and down at random. Most of them collapsed around ten, flat on their faces, moaning, gasping.

Watching them, Kate suppressed a sigh of despair. She'd been counting on this class to become a sterling reflection of her leadership abilities. And what did she have? Forty couch potatoes. She'd put in for an important promotion the week before, and the administration had her under close scrutiny. If she made the grade, she would be the first woman executive training adviser in the history of the academy. There were already mumblings that she was too young at twenty-nine, too ambitious, that she was reaching beyond her grasp. She wanted badly to prove them wrong.

Kate knew only too well the advantages and disadvantages of her unique position at Pacific. The only woman D.I. currently on staff, she was the fastest clocked female runner on the academy's obstacle course and she held several marksmanship records. Those distinctions had brought recognition to the academy and had impressed the administration. But they'd also set her up as a "top gun," of sorts, a target not unlike some of the gunslingers of the old West. In the past too many of the recruits, primarily male, had seen her as *the one to beat*. It had tended to make Kate's classes tougher to handle than most and had forced her to prove herself an effective instructor again and again. *But not this time, please,* she thought.

"Recover!" she called out. As row after row of red, puffing and puzzled faces looked up at her, she couldn't quite suppress a smile. "That means you can take your seats," she said, trying not to let her empathy become too obvious. She remembered her months of "recruit hell" vividly—the stress, the terror of failure, the physical exhaustion.

She waited until they were all in their seats. "Do we understand each other now?" she asked quietly.

"Yes, ma'am," they said in unison.

In unison, yet? Kate was inordinately pleased, but she knew it was premature to tell them so. She scanned the room, silently congratulating her recruits on getting it together so fast—and herself on winning the first round.

Her brief inspection locked on a pair of devastating green eyes, and Kate felt her senses sharpen. Set against the bronzed angularity of masculine features, this man's eyes held none of the fear and grudging respect Kate had come to expect from first-night recruits. They shimmered with curiosity—male-type curiosity. High cheekbones and rich, sable hair suggested that he might have a strain of American Indian blood, or perhaps Mexican, somewhere in his background. He looked to be in his mid-thirties, and his posture suggested he was going to be trouble. Slung low in the chair, he was resting a booted foot on his knee, and the angle of his head signaled inbred arrogance.

A warning flag went up in Kate's mind. What now? Did she have another macho hotshot on her hands? The recruits were still in their civvies, and this man's clothes looked expensive: a sheepskin jacket, stone-washed jeans, distressed leather boots. She was reasonably sure he wasn't the one who had whistled. The chiseled pride set into his mouth told her he wouldn't resort to sophomoric pranks to get attention. But he was trouble, nonetheless. *Go ahead, lady cop, take me on for size,* his eyes challenged.

"Eyes, front!" Kate barked, and the room snapped to attention. "Hands on the desk, feet on the floor!" She knew from bitter experience that it took only one rebel to disrupt an entire class.

Her breathing eased as the man moved to do what she said—not as quickly as the others, but without any real show of rebellion. He dropped his foot to the floor and set his hands on the desk, palms down, with a deliberateness in his movements. The glint was still apparent in his eyes, as though he had decided to play along. *Sure, why not,* his faint smile said.

Kate sensed that the battle lines had been drawn. He wasn't going to oppose her openly, not yet anyway, but in the meantime, he wasn't going to make things easy. And he wasn't here to become a reserve police officer. She would bet her next paycheck on that.

She glanced around the room, registering the expectant faces, the tension. "As you were," she said, nodding, and a collective sigh went up as forty recruits settled back in their chairs. Round Two, she thought, forcing her attention onto the next phase of the orientation session. This was the part she liked best, inspiring the recruits, motivating them. She called it her "fire 'em up" speech.

"Many applied for this program," she said, walking up and down the rows as she talked, "but only a few were chosen. You people are that select few. You're here because the academy believes you've got the stuff to complete this course. That's the good news. The bad news is we're tough here at Pacific. We expect—no, we *demand*—150 percent. There'll be times when you'll think you've died and gone to hell.''

She went on, detailing the rigors that lay ahead of them. Purposely she walked along the back wall of the classroom, behind the recruits, her gaze on the man with the green eyes as she paced and talked. His boot was resting on his knee again, his arm cocked along the back of the chair, but there was nothing casual about the tautness in his profile. He knew she was studying him.

Who was he? Kate asked herself. Why was he here? She'd been in her office before class going through the recruits' files when Tommy Haggerty, her coinstructor, had interrupted her to talk about some last-minute changes in the schedule. Unfortunately, Kate had never gotten back to her paperwork.

Promising herself she would pore over those damn files the first chance she got, Kate forced her full attention back to her presentation. ''This isn't fun and games, ladies and gentlemen,'' she went on, turning up an aisle and watching the recruits straighten as she moved through their ranks. ''Police work is a life-and-death matter. You'll learn to drive a police car, handle a gun and defend yourself without weapons....'' Throwing her energy into the words, Kate put the problem recruit out of her mind and the class followed her lecture with interest.

Because of all her skill in quickly sizing people up, Kate Madigan didn't realize how wrong she was about that green-eyed recruit. Not about his being trouble. He was, but not in the way she suspected. His name was Ty Raphaell, and she'd been off by an entire continent on his background. He wasn't American Indian or Mexican. His father was French, his mother Portuguese, and she'd been equally wrong about the inbred arrogance. Ty wasn't cocky, although most people thought so. He was one of those fortunate few who didn't suffer from any deficiency of self-esteem. Like Kate, he was good at what he did. Like Kate, he'd come up the hard way, achieving rather astounding success despite modest beginnings. Like Kate, he was a trailblazer, a hard driver, a loner. In all of Kate's assumptions about him, she'd scored a hit with only one. Ty had no intention of becoming a reserve officer. He was in the program for different reasons, personal reasons.

Kate continued to walk through the classroom, outlining the eighteen-week program, and finally it was his aisle that led her back to the front of the class. Moving past him, she could feel his eyes on her...and now she was the one who knew she was being watched. The realization triggered a flash of self-consciousness. Suddenly she was aware of the way she was walking, of every step she took. A tingle of nerves went up her spine.

Ty Raphaell caught the stiffening of Sergeant Madigan's shoulders as she moved past him, but he didn't register it as nerves at that moment. He was distracted by the sight of his drill instructor's backside, especially the muscles that came into play when she walked. Talk about your hard bodies, he thought, his mouth tightening to control a smile. Head to toe, she was as toned and supple as a professional athlete. A pleasant tautness surged in his thighs as she strode away from him, and he let the sensation ride for a while. He hadn't counted on a beautiful D.I. when he'd decided to take this course. Not that it would change anything, he told himself...except to make his plans more interesting.

She turned to face the class and hesitated, as though summoning her thoughts. Watching her, Ty sensed she might be unsure of herself. He wanted to think she was, at least a little. He admired strength in a woman, but it was the mystery, the quick, random glimpses of vulnerability that fascinated him.

"You'll learn a lot about yourself in the course of this training," she said, her voice softening, stirring in a way that riveted everyone's attention, "just as I did when I went through it. You'll discover who you are—and who you can be. You each had your own motives for signing up. I'll be very clear about what *my* motives are—" she stopped a moment, long enough to meet the eyes of the recruits closest to her before she looked up and acknowledged them all "—I want this to be the best damn class that ever graduated from Pacific Academy."

The murmurs arose spontaneously. As the class's response turned into sporadic clapping, Ty found himself clapping, too. She'd made a hell of an impression on all of them, including him. He was a man who liked to be surprised, and this was a woman who had surprises in store. She was more complex than she appeared, he suspected, full of pride and probably passionate as hell underneath that rigid exterior. It was the sparks in her eyes that gave her away, a vitality that seemed at odds with the controlled lines of her mouth.

She held up her hands to quiet the class, but the clapping escalated and suddenly she smiled. The recruits smiled, too, and laughed. A relaxation of tension flowed through the room.

Ty found himself studying her angular facial features. The finely drawn bones gave her a lean, spare beauty, but what would happen if her russet hair was released from its French knot? Would she look younger? Definitely. Innocent? Perhaps. Sexy? *Yes, sexy as hell.*

"Any questions?" Kate asked as the clapping subsided.

"Yeah," one of the young male recruits blurted, "what's a massive babe like you doing in a job like this?"

Ty heard a collective gasp go up, and he waited with the rest of them to see what she would do. If her own confidence in her authority was solid, she wouldn't come down hard on the kid, he reasoned. This was her chance to make some points, to win some loyalties.

"What's your name, recruit?" Kate asked.

"Jackson, ma'am." He blinked nervously.

"You really want to know why I'm here?"

"Yes, ma'am."

Kate allowed a smile to creep back into her stern expression. "I'm here to do the impossible, Jackson. They actually expect me to turn a pop-off like you into a reserve police officer."

As laughter rose again, Kate held up her hand and called out over the noise. "Class is dismissed. Take a ten-minute break and be back at the Grinder at 1900 hours suited up for inspection. You can change in the locker rooms. And look sharp, ladies and gentlemen."

As the class rose and made for the exits, Kate found herself watching the man who had distracted her all evening. By the way he'd been folded up at his desk, she had known he would be tall, and she'd sensed the lone-wolf quality so it didn't surprise her that he stood apart from the others. What did surprise her as he hung back, letting the other recruits flow through the doors, was that he seemed to be observing them. She reflected on what that might mean, but not for long, because even from across the room, his physicality came as a shock—the breadth of his shoulders, the narrowness of his hips. Conservatively speaking, he was put together like an original Olympic athlete—one of those legendary men who raced with the gods.

And then it happened. Kate just couldn't help herself. In her mind she began fitting him out in Class A khakis. It had been a long time since a man in uniform had stirred Kate

Madigan's interest, but she knew instantly this man was going to be something to behold.

Standing on the periphery of the Grinder—the dreaded slab of asphalt used for drills and inspections—Kate watched with mounting despair as her rookies returned from their break. Had her pep talk worn off already? It was 1900 hours, and yet less than half the recruits were in formation beneath the Grinder's overhead lights. The rest were straggling back in small packs, laughing, joking.

"Looks like you've got your hands full, Storm."

The gravelly male voice came from behind, and Kate knew immediately who it was. Only one man called her Storm, short for Storm Trooper, the tag she'd been given by her first class of cadets.

"Yeah, but a handful of what?" she asked, turning and staring up at the Grim Reaper smile of Tommy Haggerty, the man who had trained her ten years before.

"It *was* an interesting opening session," she admitted, suppressing relieved laughter. She didn't want it to show, but she'd never been so glad to see anyone as she was "Terrible Tommy." The class break had given her just enough time to realize that she was shaken up, and Tommy's grizzled strength would be welcome in getting through the inspection. First nights were always pandemonium.

Tommy's eyes narrowed. "Something wrong?" He glanced over her head at the rookies. "Did these squirrels give you a hard time tonight?"

"No—no, of course not," she insisted. "It was a long session, that's all. You know how first nights go." She turned around to face the recruits and groaned. They were clowning and jostling for position like high school kids. A couple of practical jokers were snapping belts, and one trained seal was balancing his hat on his nose. "Where did I go wrong?" she lamented.

"You became a D.I.," Tommy answered, laughing softly.

Kate looked up at him and wished she could take all this as casually as he did. It was so easy for Tommy. With his raspy bark and Dirty Harry grimace, he could snap Godzilla to attention. Not so for Kate Madigan. She had to *win* respect, whereas Tommy seemed naturally to command it. Kate knew the issue was complicated by her age, her looks and the fact that she was a woman training primarily men. She'd never let any of that stop her before and she wasn't about to now. Still, tonight she felt . . . uneasy.

"Let's shape up these squirrels," Tommy muttered.

"Right," she agreed, walking with him toward the disorderly bunch.

"Fall in!" Tommy barked.

Forty startled rookies froze where they stood, their ranks in serious disarray. The trained seal's hat plummeted to the ground. When he tried to catch it, he slammed into the recruit to his right and the row went down like dominoes.

"What are you, *Brownies*?" Kate bellowed. *"Boy Scouts?* Don't you know the command to attention? Form three ranks and face front. *Now*, you knuckleheads!"

The mad scramble that ensued was a scene right out of the movie *Police Academy*. Goodbye promotion, Kate thought dismally. "Dress, right, *dress*!" she blasted.

About half the recruits' left arms flew up, and their heads snapped to the right. Others extended their right arms, a few saluted and two did a neat about-face.

"Eyes front!" Tommy ordered incredulously. "Didn't any of you read your Procedures Manual?" He cut off their sheepish excuses with a disgusted wave of his hand, and then he pointed to Kate. "Sergeant Madigan here will give you turkeys one—and *only* one—demonstration of correct drill position, so watch her like she's the *last* thing you're ever going to see on this earth, because she just might be!"

Kate demonstrated and the rookies followed suit. When they finally had themselves in a reasonable facsimile of drill formation, Kate and Tommy walked through the rows, dressing down every recruit whose uniform wasn't Procedure Manual perfect.

Kate stepped in front of a young woman whose curly red hair and wide blue eyes made her look as though she'd barely made the minimum age requirement of eighteen. Her nameplate said Melissa MacGregor.

"Did you read your manual, MacGregor?" Kate asked. Every recruit had been issued a manual upon acceptance and they were supposed to have read the entire 150 pages by tonight, but Kate knew from experience that half of them wouldn't even have cracked the cover.

"Yes, ma'am," MacGregor said.

"Read it again. Your shoes are scuffed, your nameplate's crooked, and your tie bar's off by a quarter inch. The lower edge lines up with your pocket button. Got that, MacGregor?"

"Yes, ma'am."

Kate took a step back and belted out a warning to the whole platoon. "Next time I see a crooked nameplate, it'll cost the offender thirty push-ups! Is that clear?"

"Yes, ma'am!"

Kate moved on, but the young woman's image stayed in her mind. MacGregor's eyes had a certain spark to them, but the recruit had looked too slightly built to stand up to the rigors of training. Beyond that she'd reminded Kate of someone, but Kate couldn't put her finger on who it was. MacGregor's was another file she was going to have to check out at the first opportunity.

As Kate reached the last row, she slowed down deliberately. The green-eyed loner held the extreme right flank position, and Kate wanted to be ready for him when she got there.

Her voice tightened with a snap as she dressed down one recruit for the set of his hat and another for lint on his shoulders, ever aware that she was drawing closer to an unpredictable adversary. It disturbed her how much this man had taken hold of her attention, and on some level she knew that she needed to prove to herself that he was just another recruit, that she could handle him.

Finally, standing in front of him, she realized three things: according to his nameplate, his name was Ty Raphaell, his green eyes were fringed by long, dark lashes much too sensual for a man…and his uniform was *flawless*. She couldn't find one damn thing out of whack. His shoes were spit-shined to a high gloss, his pants were neatly creased and his tie hung to exactly three inches above his belt.

She scanned him up and down again, a little embarrassed at the intensity of her scrutiny as she checked to see that his shirt buttons, belt buckle and fly were all aligned. He had to have been in the military, she thought—that was the only thing that could account for this kind of perfection.

Searching, she checked the angle at which his feet were spread. "You call that forty-five degrees, Raphaell?"

He broke attention to glance down at her. "Yes, ma'am, I do," he said.

There was a shimmer of movement beneath the brilliant green of his eyes, and the dark veil of his lashes was stunning. Up close, he was the most breathtaking man Kate had ever seen. *No contest*. Baffled by his break of position, she found herself wondering what she was supposed to say next—until she heard Tommy bellowing, "Eyes *front*, Raphaell!"

Kate snapped back to attention, astonished that she'd allowed such a lapse of procedure. "Head *erect*, Raphaell!" she bit out, automatically launching into an intense scrutiny of his attention stance. "Chin up, chest out, shoulders square!"

She moved past him, pivoted and looked him up and down, aware that she had to get control of herself. "Your hands, recruit," she said, noticing that he'd curled them into fists. "Did you read your manual?"

"Yes, ma'am."

There was no denying the huskiness of his voice or the unsteadiness in her own. "What does it say about the position of the hands, Raphaell?" she demanded.

"The tip of the thumb touches the tip of the forefinger, *ma'am*."

"Do it, Raphaell."

Kate watched as his hands began to slowly uncurl, and she felt a strange and opposite sensation in her stomach, as if a spring was recoiling to its proper tension. Her own mother had always blithely claimed that all a man needed were good hands and a good job to keep a woman happy. This guy has the hands part covered, she thought, sure she'd never seen anything quite so sensual as the way his thumb and forefinger came together, just touching. Nerves sparked again, in her stomach this time, as startling as the *ching* of metal against glass.

What's *happening* to me? she wondered, frozen.

With a sharp glance at Raphaell to make sure he wasn't smiling, she executed a right-face and marched to the front of the platoon. Her heart was pounding and Tommy was staring at her oddly, but she shook her head as though nothing had happened.

As she turned to face the recruits, her eyes riveting on Raphaell, a thought flashed through her mind: nothing like that had ever happened to her before and, by God, it would never happen again.

Chapter Two

Owwee! Arrest me, please,'' a male voice warbled as Kate entered the noisy confines of Mother's, a local watering hole that Tommy Haggerty frequented. Kate turned to her right and saw "Slam" Schumacher waving at her, a local rowdy who spent so much time at Mother's she suspected he'd taken up residence. There were several other unsavory types at Slam's table, all grinning at her.

"Don't tempt me, Slam," Kate warned, dismissing him as she searched the bar's murky, smoke-filled interior for Tommy. She reminded herself to ask Tommy why he hung out at this place instead of the Tradewinds, a Polynesian cocktail lounge where the other drill instructors "convened" after class. But then why ask? she thought. Tommy's answer would be something to the effect that drinks with straws and umbrellas were a crime against nature and good rum. Tommy never was one to *go along*, a trait Kate found particularly ironic since Tommy's job was, among other things, training recruits to follow orders without hesitation.

Kate spotted the lanky, weathered drill instructor at the bar, silently finishing off a mug of dark beer. Ignoring Slam's whistles, she crossed the room to join Tommy.

"Hi, partner." She slid onto a bar stool.

"Hey, Storm," he said, grinning. "When I last saw you, you were in your office doing an imitation of a dutiful drill instructor."

"If you mean I was going over the recruits' files, you're right. But it had more to do with self-preservation than it did with duty—I think we may have a problem on our hands with one of the rookies. Coors Lite," she called out as the bartender looked her way.

"Yeah?" Tommy said, only mildly interested. "Which one?"

"Raphaell."

Tommy leaned into the arm he'd propped on the bar and rubbed his forehead thoughtfully. "Raphaell? Let's see... tall, dark hair, mid-thirties?"

"Thirty-six, six-two, and according to his stats, he's an attorney."

"Is that the problem?"

"Well... maybe. I don't know. There's too much about him that doesn't jibe. Why is he taking the training? His bio says he's retired from law. It says he's a writer and a teacher. Does that make sense to you? Retired at thirty-six?"

"It makes a lot more sense than working your behind off till you're sixty-five. Besides, we've had attorneys enrolled before. We've had plumbers, doctors, ministers."

She caught the ice-cold glass of beer the bartender slid her way and nodded her thanks. "Yeah, but this guy is different, Tommy. I think we've got a problem on our hands. His attitude—"

Tommy lifted an eyebrow skeptically. "We've got a problem? Or *you've* got a problem? What are you so uptight about? If the guy's pushing around some attitude, we'll push it back."

Kate exhaled an uneasiness she didn't quite understand and took a sip of beer. Its tangy bubbles burned her throat, hot and cold at once. She decided not to mention the file reference she'd found regarding Raphaell's two-year stint in the army. There was nothing unusual about it, and a military background was generally considered a plus in law enforcement. "I just wish I knew why he wanted to be a reserve police officer," she mumbled, more to herself than to Tommy.

"If you ask me," Tommy observed, "it's that kid MacGregor you ought to be worrying about. She's not a hundred pounds, dripping wet."

"MacGregor's all right," Kate defended, ignoring the fact that she'd had the same reservations. "I can see it in her eyes, Tommy. She's motivated."

Tommy rolled the beer mug in his hands and glanced her way. "She's a kid, Kate. She hasn't got the stuff."

"Oh *God*," Kate said, laughing, suddenly remembering who Melissa MacGregor reminded her of. "That's exactly what you said to me ten years ago. *Ten years ago!* Do you remember, Tommy? You set me down in your office and told me you'd thrown back bigger fish than me. You said I was too young, too damn skinny and you told me to come back when I had a pair of—"

"Shoulders," he cut in, deadpan. "I said shoulders, and I still think I was right."

"Yeah, well, thank God I knew you weren't. Look at me, Haggerty. I'm twenty-nine, I'm a police sergeant, a D.I. and I still haven't got shoulders."

"Yes, but you sure got a mouth," he muttered.

"I learned from the best," she came back.

Their sidelong glances were fierce and fond, just like their relationship. As the standoff subsided into low laughter, Kate decided it was time to tell him something she'd been putting off for days. "I guess you heard that Art's leaving at the end of this class." She meant Arthur Buchanan, one of the academy's executive training advisers and hers and Tommy's supervisor.

Tommy nodded. "Blood pressure problems, right?"

"I guess the job finally got to him. I've put in for the position," she added quickly.

Tommy blinked and took a quick gulp of his beer. It was the most emotion Kate had seen him show in their five years of working together.

"Now why would you want to be an executive training adviser?" he asked. "You got the itch for power?"

Kate knew how Tommy felt about executive and management positions. He disliked careerism and politics in any form, and he claimed power playing was rampant in the upper echelons.

"It has nothing to do with power, Tommy. I want to do the job better, that's all. I also want to do it because nobody thinks I can." She heard the intensity in her own voice and realized how important the position had become to her. "Listen, how bad could I be?" she said, hoping to win him over with humor. "You trained me, right?"

He shrugged, then finished off his beer. "And I'll be around to keep you from getting too big for your khakis. You can bet the rent on that."

"So...what? You think it's a good idea?"

He glanced at her and grinned. "I think it's a lousy idea, but then I think most everything's a lousy idea—except fly fishing off the Colorado River. Good luck, Storm."

Kate's relieved smile faded as Tommy's eyes narrowed. "Speak of the devil," he said, looking over her shoulder.

"Art Buchanan's here?" she questioned. "At Mother's?"

"No. It's your attitude problem—Raphaell." Tommy dug a bill out of his pocket and dropped it on the bar. "Looks like now's your chance."

"Chance for what?"

"To find out why he's in the program." Tommy slid off the stool and zipped up his jacket.

"Where're you going?" Kate asked, a trace of panic in her voice. "I can't talk to him here. You know how the academy feels about fraternization."

"I'm not talking about fraternizing, Storm, I'm talking about counseling. That's what the academy pays you to do, isn't it? So, counsel this guy. Find out what he's got in mind. As for me, I'm going home to a turkey TV dinner and reruns on the tube."

Kate swallowed the objection on her lips as Tommy gave her a thumbs-up and shouldered past her to leave. Mother's was hardly the place to counsel recruits. She'd changed into jeans and a sweater to come here, and without her uniform and her office she felt at a distinct disadvantage. God, the symbols of power, she thought. Was Tommy's crackerbarrel philosophy right? Were uniforms and batons and guns just props? "If you haven't got it in here, you haven't got it," he always said, pointing to his gut.

Kate glanced around and saw Tommy stop for a brief word with the recruit on his way out the door. Oddly, she sensed a grudging respect in Tommy's demeanor. Raphaell was wearing the sheepskin jacket and jeans he'd had on during the orientation session, and he didn't look any more like a lawyer now than he had then. Perhaps Tommy sensed another nonconformist, a kindred spirit. Whatever it was, the drill instructor finished his brief conversation with the recruit and left.

Kate straightened on the bar stool as Raphaell spotted her. Everything seemed to quicken at once—her breathing, her heart rate, even her throat felt a little dry. She subdued the reaction with a deep breath and a supreme effort of will, then stared back at him as he walked toward her. As always when challenged, she felt an inner resolve mobilizing. Indomitable spirit, her Irish police captain grandfather used to call it. And he also used to say that pubs were the next best thing to confessionals for finding out what you wanted to know about people.

"Permission to sit, ma'am," Ty said, indicating the empty stool next to her.

Kate caught the irony in his voice and the shimmer of something electric in his green eyes. There was a subtle force in his nearness that took a moment to get used to, like the sudden tug of a wave you weren't expecting. "I think we can forgo the instructor/recruit formalities just this once," she conceded wryly. "By all means, sit down."

Ty signaled the bartender, ordered himself a Scotch and water. "You come here often?" he asked casually, turning to Kate.

"No, not often." There is *nothing* casual about this man, she thought, struck by the complex signals he gave off. The energy in his eyes, the laughter in his voice, gave the impression that every question, even the one he'd just asked, had a hidden meaning. If this were a card game they were playing, she would have sworn he'd already seen her hand.

Glancing over her shoulder, she looked around Mother's and back at him, determined to match his surface cool. "Not exactly the place you'd expect to find a cop—is that what you're thinking?"

"I was thinking this is exactly the sort of place I'd expect to find a cop like Haggerty... but not a woman like you."

Kate took a sip of her beer and swallowed it with some difficulty. A woman like *me*? she thought. What the heck did that mean? She knew better than to ask the question and be led into the sort of intimacy the answer promised. "If Mother's is good enough for Tommy," she said lightly, "then it's good enough for me."

"I see," he said, laughing, tilting his glass until the ice clinked. "So that's how it is with you and Haggerty."

"It's none of your business how *anything* is with me and *Sergeant* Haggerty, Raphaell."

In the snap of silence that followed, Kate felt a nerve spasm in her throat. Firecracker-angry, she barely held back a lecture on the danger of jumping to conclusions. Who did he think he was, anyway, speculating on her relationships?

It was the surprise on his face that told her she might be overreacting. She felt the heat subside slightly, and with the cooling effect came an instant of embarrassed self-awareness. God, she'd almost lost it. She was on edge in this place and around him, but that was no excuse for chewing his ear off—even if he *was* off base. Kate knew only too well that people lost control when they were angry. Her Irish temper had always been her downfall during childhood, but she had thought she'd finally mastered it.

"Ah, I guess we're back in the recruit/instructor mode," Ty observed quietly.

A much safer mode to be in with this man, she thought. "Not necessarily—"

He turned to look at her, and Kate saw the same question in his eyes that had passed through her mind. Just what mode were they in?

"If I implied something I shouldn't have, I'm sorry." The amusement was gone from his eyes and his voice.

"Forget it." Still simmering, Kate picked up her mug with both hands and linked her fingers around it. This entire idea had been a mistake and she knew it. One of Tommy's mistakes, she reminded herself, and she had every intention of telling him so when she saw him.

She'd just about decided to fold her tent and slink away when Raphaell surprised her with another question.

"There's a rumor going around that your nickname is Storm Trooper? What did you do to earn that?"

Kate looked up at him. "Stick out the course. You'll find out."

His shoulders moved with suppressed laughter. "Best offer I've had all day."

"Really? I'm sorry to hear that."

"Watch it," he warned her. "I'm a sucker for sympathy."

Kate felt herself softening—and reflecting on what an intriguing smile he had. Much as she might have liked to deny it, there was simply no missing this man's underlying intensity, his intelligence. And those qualities intimidated Kate a little. Strength and character she had plenty of—though no one would have guessed it if they'd caught her in this raunchy bar drinking with a recruit. But intelligence, well, she'd never thought of herself as genius material.

Staring at him, she asked the question that had brought her to Mother's to talk to Tommy. "What are you doing at the academy, Raphaell?"

His eyes narrowed, glimmering with devilishness. "You must be a riot at parties. Are you always this point-blank?"

"If you want to hit, you've got to aim. That's what my grandpop used to say." Actually, Kate's directness varied according to her insecurities. In really threatening situations, she was a machine gun.

"Your grandpop sounds like a man I'd like to have had on my side," Ty admitted. "Listen, I have a feeling this isn't the answer you're looking for, but I signed up for the same reason the other recruits did—to take the reserve officer training."

"You really want to be a reserve cop? Why?"

"To protect, defend and serve?"

Kate didn't need to be a genius to know that she was being put on. His style, full of subtle and evasive irony, was charming, and particularly frustrating to a woman who dealt in rapid-fire questions and answers. "You're going to be a handful, Raphaell. I can see that."

"I sure hope so."

The look in his eyes provoked a response in Kate that was completely inappropriate in a drill instructor. As his gaze drifted from her eyes to her mouth and her breasts, just that deliberately, just that sensually, a sensation spread through her that revved her senses like an adrenaline rush. And what startled her most was that she liked it, all of it—the tingly warmth, the acute awareness of herself, of him, the glimmer of apprehension that was beginning to evidence itself. Suddenly she felt plugged into a direct current.

"God, what a sight," he said.

"What? Me?" She glanced down at the V-neck sweater she had on and looked up at him, confused.

"You...blushing. Or whatever that rosy glow is all about. It's stunning."

Kate touched her face, registering its warmth, and astonished laughter bubbled. Sergeant Madigan blushing? Had the world gone crazy? Suddenly she was glad she'd worn civilian clothes and taken her red hair out of its "official police business" bun. Suddenly she was glad she was here, that *he* was here.

It was the feelings sweeping up from her toes that provided Kate with this unexpected information, not the commentary in her head. Her thoughts had something altogether different in mind. What's going on, Madigan? they questioned, loudly. The voice of Kate Madigan's conscience was a force unto itself. Never retiring, never equivocal, it sounded very much like her grandfather. *What's this all about, Madigan?*

This man is flirting with me, Kate answered the voice without thinking. He's flirting with me. *And I like it.*

Ty was studying her with the intent look of a man whose curiosity was becoming sexual. "Do I get the next question?" he asked.

"Sure," Kate said, looking away. The awkwardness of it hit her all at once, and suddenly she became preoccupied with a snag in one of her fingernails.

"What are *you* doing at the academy?"

She laughed but kept her gaze on the beer mug in front of her. "I have a feeling this isn't the answer you're looking for, either, but I work there. My bosses wouldn't like it very much if I didn't show up."

"But why police work? Why training recruits? Do you actually *like* that kind of work?"

The tone of disbelief in his voice surprised her. Turning the mug in her hands, she said, "If you mean, do I like ordering people around, the answer is no. I don't particularly like that part of it. But I like inspiring the recruits to do their best. And I like the pride in their eyes when they succeed."

"I can believe that."

She glanced his way then, expecting the gentle, teasing smile, but it wasn't there.

"So... are you happy?" he asked.

"Happy?" It was an unexpected question, and Kate just stared at him a moment. "You can get pretty point-blank yourself."

"Just watch me." He grinned, the upper lip curling faintly at one corner, the bottom lip full, smooth.

The mouth of a sensualist, Kate thought. That was the word that described him better than any other, she realized, with his dusky skin tone, his heavily lashed eyes and the slow, wanton quality of his smile.

"Well," he persisted, "what is it? Happy? Unhappy? The world is waiting."

She hadn't thought about whether she was happy or not in years. No answer came to mind, nothing at all. "I get by," she said finally.

"Not an unqualified endorsement for police work," he observed.

"Police work is the happiest part of my life," she said, and immediately wished she hadn't. It was too personal, too revealing. It was an invitation to probe further, into things she couldn't talk about, *wouldn't* talk about. "Let's change the subject, Raphaell."

She took another sip of the beer and found it flat, acrid. As the taste lingered in her mouth, a question came to mind. If this was a counseling session, exactly who was counseling whom? She had no business being here, talking to this man, feeling things for this man. God, it was so easy to forget he was one of her recruits. Just being with him could get her into trouble professionally—and in so many *other* ways.

Through Kate's thoughts, she heard Ty ordering her another beer. "No, I have to go," she said, pushing the glass away.

"Is something wrong?"

She slid off the stool and bent to find her purse on the floor. As she stood up, he stopped her with a hand on her forearm.

"Where're you going?" he asked.

His touch was pressureless but somehow possessive, as though he thought he had the right to question her, as though she was . . . what? His woman? Of course he didn't think that. He couldn't think *that*. But Kate couldn't shake the image. She felt her heart pounding, and the warmth swept through her again. "Let go of me, Raphaell. That's an order."

"Must be convenient as hell to have those orders to hide behind," he said, his voice low, "not to mention the uniform, the badge, the gun?"

He loosened his hold without letting go of her, and Kate, for some reason she didn't understand, did not pull free. Maybe it was the feel of his skin against hers, the strength of his hand. Maybe it was the fact that she hadn't been touched this intimately, possessively, by a man in so many years; not once, not even a hand held in a movie. Or maybe it was his radiant green eyes and the things they were saying to her—that she was beautiful, desirable. Was that what they were saying? Or was that what she wanted them to say? She felt a kind of pain rise inside her, sharp and sweet, like a haunting chord of music. Pierced by an emotion she barely understood, she said, "Let go of me, *please*. I have to go."

He released her then, silently, without apology and turned back to his drink.

Kate rushed through the noisy confusion of the bar, flinching as she passed Slam, his gang of lowlife friends and their jeering remarks. She stumbled just as she reached the entrance and lurched forward, her shoulder colliding with the heavy wooden door.

"Take a look at that broad," someone hooted. "She's pie-eyed."

Embarrassed, furious with herself, Kate caught her balance and pushed through the swinging door. She burst out into the cool spring night and hurried across the parking lot toward her car. Glancing around the area out of habit, she fished through her purse for her key chain. The miniature metal baton attached to a brass key ring was the only weapon she carried.

She was fitting the key into the car door when she heard the crunch of gravel underfoot.

"Yo, gorgeous."

Kate swung around to see Slam Schumacher coming across the lot toward her.

"You have a fight with your boyfriend?" he called out. "'Cause if you're looking for somebody to fill in tonight, I just happen to be free."

"I'm not looking, Slam," she said, realizing by his walk that he was just drunk enough to be trouble. She pulled open the car door and tossed her bag inside, freeing herself of physical restrictions in case he couldn't be talked into behaving himself.

"Ah, come on," he said, nearing her. "We could have some fun. Nobody has to know."

"I'd know, Slam."

His eyes turned mean then. "What is this? I'm not good enough for the lady cop? You'd rather mix it up with half-breeds, or whatever the hell that guy is in there." He stumbled up to her, his breath reeking of alcohol.

She stepped back, keeping him at arm's length, and at the same time visually checking him for weapons. "Don't do something you'll regret, Slam. I don't want to have to take you in tonight, but I will—"

He lunged toward her, and before Kate could react a hand reached out of the darkness and closed on his shoulder. She watched in shock as Slam was jerked back, whipped around and slugged in the stomach by a blur of action in human form. As the drunken man grunted, doubled up and dropped to the ground, she saw that it was Ty Raphaell standing over him, poised aggressively, ready to finish the downed man off if he tried to get up.

"Raphaell, what are you *doing*?" Kate demanded.

Ty nudged the man with his foot, apparently to make sure that he was no longer a threat, and then he turned to Kate, searching her face. "Are you okay? Did he hurt you?"

"No, of course not. Why did you hit him?"

"Come on," he said, ignoring her question as he approached her and took her by the arm. "Let's get you out of here. This place is a dive."

Kate jerked away. "Raphaell!"

His features clouded with confusion. "What's wrong?" he said. "The guy was coming on to you. He was drunk. I was trying to help."

"I don't need *help*, Raphaell. I can help myself. I'm trained in self-defense. Look at what you've done. You assaulted the man, for God's sake."

Ty's jaw tightened. "He was coming at you. I thought you were in trouble."

Kate knew exactly what had happened. Raphaell had reacted like a man would who was trying to protect a defenseless woman. After what had happened between them in the bar, he'd forgotten that she was not only a policewoman but his D.I. *She couldn't let him forget it again.*

"I can take care of myself," she said tensely. The impulse to bark orders at him was strong. She wanted to treat him as she would have any other recruit, to tell him to get the hell home, to study for tomorrow night's class. But his remark about how easy it was to hide behind those orders stuck in her mind. Turning, she jerked the still-dangling keys from the door of the car and swung into the front seat.

He stepped out of her way as she backed up the car and wheeled it around, spraying gravel as she drove off.

The pull to look back, to see if he was still watching her, was strong, but Kate wouldn't let herself do it. And suddenly that decision became a test of her will, of her self-control. Her stomach muscles tightened as she swung the car around to the exit and braked for the passing street traffic.

Her eyes locked on the road and she pulled into the flow of cars. A few blocks later she released a deep breath. She was okay. She was *fine*. And finally, pulling onto the freeway and feeling strength flow back into her, she allowed herself a faint smile. How had she let that situation get so far out of hand?

By the time she reached her apartment, the confusion was gone. Her position in relation to him was crystal clear in her mind. Kate Madigan was a drill instructor, committed to training future police officers to the best of her ability. And Ty Raphaell? He was a recruit, *nothing more*.

Chapter Three

Aware of his own labored breathing, Ty Raphaell felt the fatigue in his legs with every stride he took. The grass under his feet had begun to feel like concrete, and the tortured groans of the few rookies still slogging it out with him in Sergeant Madigan's "warm-up run" were enough to demoralize a triathlete, which he wasn't.

"Damn," he breathed, veering to avoid a collision with the heavyset recruit who'd slowed down in front of him.

Ahead of the pack, Sergeant Madigan glanced over her shoulder and saw the struggling rookie drop back and stagger to a halt. "What have I got, a platoon full of pansies?!" she bellowed, waving them on. "Keep *going*!"

She's nuts, Ty thought, realizing she had no intention of stopping. They were nearing their starting point again, the "workout yard," so named because of its functional resemblance to a prison exercise pen, but she was gearing up for another lap.

"How many miles is that, ma'am?" the platoon leader, a thin wiry kid in his twenties, puffed.

"Three, but who's counting, Schnabel?" Madigan called back without a hint of fatigue in her voice.

Ty smiled grimly and moved up until he was running just behind them. He'd be damned if he was going to let a wet-behind-the-ears kid and a deranged D.I. run him into the ground. Controlling his breathing and slowing his arm swing, he leaned forward and put his body on automatic pilot. Time to get serious, he told himself, grateful that he'd run a few 10K races over the years.

Feeling the natural rhythm of long-distance running flow back into him, he watched the woman in front of him with grim appreciation. She moved with effortless fluidity, skimming over the ground like Nike herself. With her thick auburn hair pulled up into a ponytail and her regulation blue running shorts and white T-shirt, she looked like a high school cheerleader. A man would be a fool to take that illusion too seriously, though, he reminded himself.

It was two weeks, today, since their encounter in the bar, and she'd been riding the recruits mercilessly ever since. She'd impressed them all with her stamina and sheer guts. She never asked anyone to do anything she couldn't do, and she drove that fact home again and again by outperforming every one of them—including him on more than one occasion. But she'd infuriated him, too, with her relentless demands. Sure as coyotes howled at the moon, this lady had something to prove, and he'd begun to think she was going to kill off the entire platoon doing it.

They crossed the periphery of the asphalt parking lot and two more recruits fell out, clutching their sides and heaving. Only six of us left, Ty observed sardonically. Six loyal soldiers following their demented leader into the Valley of Death-by-Blisters.

As Sergeant Madigan glanced back and saw that he was still behind her, the look in her stormy, slate-colored eyes drove one thing home. It wasn't the platoon she was trying to kill off, it was him. As hard as she'd been on the other rookies, she'd been twice as hard on him. She'd been putting him to the test daily, *hourly*, targeting him, badgering him, and he had a hunch he knew why.

He hadn't been able to resist shaking her up every once in a while with offhand comments, glances. In a subtle way he supposed he'd been challenging her to try to bring him under control, but that alone couldn't account for her reactions. It went deeper than that. She'd felt something that night in the bar, and it had scared her. So he *hadn't* imagined that flash of longing in her eyes just before she walked out. It was naked and beautiful. It had mesmerized him. With the blink of an eye, she had told him more about herself than some women revealed in the course of an entire relationship. She was hurting under that "hang tough" front of hers and the pain had exposed her, leaving her vulnerable for a moment. He had no way of knowing how long it had been since she'd been with a man, but he suspected it had been, well…too long. He also suspected she would deny any such need ferociously.

Watching her now, matching her stride for stride, it was hard to believe this was the same woman he'd been with that night. She'd smothered any hint of vulnerability under her tough D.I. facade. It probably would have bugged her if she'd realized that the fiercer she got, the more fiery and beautiful she was. *And the more she played right into his hands.*

Without realizing it, Sergeant Kate Madigan was proving his thesis. He had no intention of using her name or indicting her personally, but the fact of it was she was handing him material for his study on a platter. With any luck, he was going to open some eyes with his study on the abuses of military and police training. And though he wouldn't put Madigan in the category of an abusive D.I., she was unbelievably tough. The drop rate for her platoon was already thirty percent higher than normal for this stage of the training. Ty intended to interview a couple of those washouts when he had the chance. Right now he didn't have the energy to interview a rock! He was too busy trying to survive.

When they hit the last stretch, Ty was the only recruit still with her, and he was on the ragged edge. She, on the other hand, was striding smoothly, as though she was born to run—as though it hadn't even occurred to her that she'd left her entire class, even the platoon leader, gasping by the wayside.

What is this woman? Ty asked himself. A tribal huntress? Bionic? The last lap was rough going but he stuck it out, and as they hit the final stretch he got his second wind and pulled up alongside her.

She picked up the pace, glaring at him. "You're out of formation, Raphaell," she warned.

It was obvious she wanted him a respectful distance behind her, but he wasn't in the mood for deference. To hell with formation, he thought, staying with her.

She picked up the pace again.

He pulled up alongside her again.

"Back off, Raphaell!"

"Ma'am?"

As they reached the workout yard, she halted by the obstacle course vault and whirled on him.

"Are you *deaf*, recruit?!"

He couldn't resist. "What, ma'am?"

"That'll cost you thirty for breaking formation and fifteen more for the damn dumb joke, Raphaell. Hit the turf."

It gave him some satisfaction as he dropped to push-up position and ticked off forty-five that she'd been panting, too, and perspiring. Maybe he'd given her as good a run as she'd given him.

"Forty-five, ma'am," he breathed on the last heave. "Permission to recover?" He held the position, his arms feeling the strain of his body weight, and when she didn't respond, he looked up and saw her studying him. The damp ringlets that had pulled free from her ponytail made her look like a wayward child. The angry darts of fire in her eyes made her look like a woman capable of bringing down a charging rhino if she so chose.

"Permission to recover?" he said again, the words hissing through his teeth as he locked his elbows for support.

She walked toward him, circled him once, and when she spoke her voice was raspy.

"Your arms are going to start to shake soon, Raphaell," she said, "and then you're going to feel the burn. When that burn gets bad enough, you're going to bite the dust, recruit. Have you ever dropped, Raphaell?"

His jaw clenched in anger. He knew this was a contest of wills, and he knew she was threatened. He could hear the uncertainty in her voice, but at this point he didn't give a damn. She'd been shoveling barbs and insults at him all week, and he'd swallowed all of them, but not this one. He would remember this one. And one day—*one fine day*—she would get it back.

Within moments his arms were shaking and his biceps were on fire. The muscles in his shoulders throbbed as he fought to hold himself up. He might die, but he wouldn't drop—and he sure as *hell* wouldn't ask her for permission to recover again.

"Answer me, Raphaell. Have you ever dropped?"

"*No*, ma'am," he snarled.

"Never?" she pressed.

"Only my pants, ma'am, but I don't think you want to hear about that."

She breathed a word that would have made a linebacker blush. "*Recover*, Raphaell. On your feet."

Fighting down a blast of sheer physical anguish, he knelt on one knee and released the pressure from his palms. Pain shot up his arms like electricity. Even his bones were screaming. If it had been her goal to inflict punishment, she'd done it. If it had been her goal to infuriate him, she'd done that, too. He glared up at her and pushed to his feet, wondering what in the hell this woman's problem was.

Kate Madigan couldn't have answered that question if he'd asked it out loud. Not because the problem was so complex. In fact, it was quite simple. *She was attracted to him.* Only she didn't know that yet—not consciously, anyway. She was too busy denying it, fighting it, resisting even the notion of it—and with all her resistance, she was compounding things. She'd given so much energy to her "problem" with Raphaell that she couldn't sleep nights for thinking about it. She'd even begun to dream about him.

Kate knew Raphaell spelled trouble. She just didn't know how much trouble. Yet. In her mind he was an attitude problem. He wasn't taking her *or* the academy seriously, and it was her job to bring him into line.

The recruits straggled back, spent and spiritless, but Kate wasn't done with them yet. This was their first major workout, and it was designed to bring them face-to-face with the hard reality of academy standards and to give them a preview of what was in store. Pain, strain and perspiration, Tommy liked to call it. "Fall in!" she ordered.

First she lectured them on the benefits of physical fitness, and then she informed them point-blank that there wasn't a rookie in the platoon who could pass the physical fitness exam coming up. With a line-drive stare at Raphaell, she added, "Some of you run a little better than others, but that won't get you through the exam. You'll be tested on your speed, agility, dexterity and physical strength—*and* on your ability to quickly respond to orders."

When she finished her spiel, she put them through a battery of aerobiclike calisthenics, first demonstrating what she wanted and then scrutinizing and criticizing as they performed jumping jacks, leg raises, sit-ups and curls.

"More, I want *more*!" she yelled when they began to groan and collapse. "Let's see some major muscle action!"

"Come on, you turkeys!" she pleaded, moments later, trying to shame them into finishing the last round of sit-ups. "Give me five more for the academy!"

Glancing involuntarily at Raphaell, who'd chosen that precise moment to strip off his T-shirt, Kate quickly turned her attention to the other recruits, particularly MacGregor. The young, exceedingly slender woman was ashen and trembling as she fought desperately to make the count. She's not strong enough, Kate realized despairingly. She's got the spirit of ten recruits, but her body isn't up to it.

Several others hadn't made it, either, but Kate diagnosed them as either being out of shape or lazy. Most of them would graduate if they were willing to sweat and chew for it. But maybe Tommy was right about MacGregor. Watching the young woman struggle, Kate felt all the agony of her own first workout session. It was do or die, and finally Kate had done it. Come on, MacGregor, *do it*, she coached silently.

As the workout progressed, Kate realized how seriously out of shape her platoon was. She coached, pep-talked and even threatened them, but to no avail. Finally, aware that she was pushing them to their limit, she simply let them lie where they dropped. By the time they got to the pull-ups, the only recruit left on his feet was Ty Raphaell.

"Pull-ups, Raphaell," she warned. "You tough enough to do ten of them?"

"Yes, ma'am."

Kate nodded at him grimly, giving him the go-ahead, but secretly she didn't believe he would manage more than three—if that. Pull-ups, similar to chin-ups, but with the hands gripping the front of the bar, were torturous, a killer of men.

Sweat dripping from his body, his jaw locked in brutal determination, Ty leaped, grabbed hold of the bar and pulled himself up in a slow, savage display of brute strength. The muscles in his arms bunched painfully as he held the position, his chin at the bar, and then he lowered himself an inch at a time, and with a throttled moan, pulled himself up again. He did it ten times in all, and it was a beautiful and agonizing sight.

The entire class went silent, arrested by the power, the savagery of this man in a battle against his own physical limitations.

Kate felt her stomach knot up watching him. He was magnificent. He had more guts and raw fight in him than any recruit she'd ever trained. He wouldn't be controlled, he wouldn't be broken. He took everything she threw at him and threw it back in her face.

He dropped from the bar, hit the ground and half turned, glaring at her. Sweat streamed down the taut, ruddied muscles of his chest and abdomen and pooled at the waistband of his shorts. The hair that knifed up the center of his belly was etched against heaving sinew like dark wings. Fury flashed in his green eyes. *Satisfied, lady cop?*

Kate stared at him, her heart erratic, hating him at that moment, enthralled by him. "Good work, Raphaell," she said at last.

Turning away from him, drawing in a breath, she fought to regain control of herself. She glowered at the class, most of whom were still sprawled on the ground. "Okay, you world class wimps," she rasped, fighting to steady her voice, "fall in!"

As the recruits scrambled into formation, she laid down the law, telling them in no uncertain terms that they were a disgrace to their athletic gear. Finally, to the howling dismay of the entire class, she scheduled extra fitness classes that week—and every week—until they were up to standard.

"Get out of here, you tenderfoots," she muttered finally, glancing at her watch. "You're dismissed for lunch. Class reconvenes at 1300 hours, room 319. Be there!"

Turning away, still shaken by what had taken place, she saw Tommy walking across the field toward her, a frown knit into his expression.

"Think you might be riding the troops a little hard?" he asked as he reached her.

"Hard . . . ? But that's my *job*." Catching the ring of defensiveness in her voice, Kate shrugged. "C'mon, Tommy," she reminded him gently, "we're supposed to ride the new recruits. How else do we weed out the ones who can't take the stress—not to mention the physical demands? Aren't you the guy who taught me that *one* bad cop is too many?"

It struck Kate as darn odd that "Terrible Tommy" was calling her on the very thing that had earned him his nickname. The *administration of stress* as the academy so euphemistically called it, was one of Kate's least-loved duties. She saw the necessity for it, but she had never relished it. That was Tommy's arena. And now he was telling her she was being too tough?

"I'd hate to think this has something to do with that promotion you're up for, Storm," he said, crooking an eyebrow.

"The promotion?" It hit her then that he thought she was pushing the recruits because she wanted to look good, to impress the academy. Was he right? Wiping away the sweat that was trickling down her temple, she shook her head.

"This is not about the promotion, Tommy." She wasn't quite as sure of that statement as she sounded, but a crack drill instructor didn't equivocate. That much of her training, at least, seemed to have stuck.

"What's going on, then?" he questioned.

"What makes you think something's going on?" Kate usually confided in Tommy, but this time she had the feeling he might not understand. Especially since she wasn't sure how to articulate the problem—or even what it was exactly.

"You've been driving your rookies into the ground like so many fence posts, that's what's going on. Sure looks like you've got something to prove to somebody. If it's not the administration, then it wouldn't be that problem recruit, would it? Raphaell?"

She met Tommy's steely gaze, and a hot denial twitched on her lips. Coloring, she realized that if Tommy was right, if she was riding roughshod, it had more to do with Raphaell than with the promotion.

"Yes, I *am* having some problems with him, but nothing that can't be handled. And I don't think I'm being too tough on the recruits, Tommy. You've seen them. Not one of them could pass the fitness qualifier if I gave it today."

"Except Raphaell," he pointed out.

Kate's scalp tightened. Yes, dammit, he *could* pass the exam. He could probably fly if he made up his mind to. "That's not the issue with him," she countered. "I'm still not convinced he's officer material, Tommy. *Or* that he's taking this program seriously."

"You were going to have a little talk with him at Mother's a couple of weeks ago, weren't you?" Tommy observed, eyeing her thoughtfully. "What happened? Now that I think about it, you never mentioned it."

Kate held the breath she'd just taken for a moment. "Nothing really. I had a little trouble with Slam Schumacher when I left, and Raphaell decided to play the white knight. I set him straight, that's all.''

Tommy was staring at her as if he could see through every camouflage barrier her mind threw up. Finally he lifted a shoulder and changed the subject. "If you're saying there's no problem, there's no problem. What about that other recruit, MacGregor? How's she coming around?''

"Slowly," Kate admitted, feeling a stab of guilt. She wasn't ready to admit to Tommy that he might have been right about MacGregor. She wanted to talk to the recruit first, give her every possible chance to make it. "She's a featherweight, but I think, I *hope*, she's got enough spirit and stamina to compensate for the lack of strength. And she's bright—brighter than anyone else in the class." *Except Raphaell*, she heard herself adding silently, and she could see by Tommy's expression that he'd done the same.

"Lunch?" he said, typically brusque. "I've got some Alka-Seltzer on me. How about a chili dog at Barnie's?''

"No thanks, I'm going to shower up—'' she smiled at him, her way of acknowledging that maybe he'd been right "—and do some thinking." With that she patted his arm and took off for the women's locker room.

"Forty-*five*," Kate gasped, completing the last push-up and locking her arms in the hold position. Glancing around the campus gym to make sure she was still alone, she began mentally counting off the seconds. It surprised her how quickly the burning began in her shoulders. It flared down her arms, and then the shaking started. She let out a muffled groan and clenched her teeth, certain her wrists were about to snap.

She hadn't planned to end up in the gym doing push-ups. She'd gone to the locker room with every intention of taking a shower, cooling down and bringing things into perspective. She still wasn't convinced Tommy was right about her overzealousness, but he *was* right about her nerves. She was jumpy. Even the extended run hadn't burned off her nervous energy. That's when she'd begun to wonder whether she could hold the position as long as Raphaell had.

"Or *longer*," she groaned, letting out a low moan of agony. As long as she was here, she was going for the record.

"You building triceps? Or character?" an amused male voice inquired.

"Raphaell?" Kate gasped, hearing him come up behind her, "what are you doing here?"

"I came to talk."

Kate dropped to her knees and hunched that way for a minute, her muscles knotted with pain. *Maybe if I keep my eyes shut, he'll go away.*

"Need a hand?" he asked.

"Need a hand, *what*?" She was asking for a *ma'am*, the required term of respect. When he didn't answer, she twisted around and glared up at him. If there was anything more embarrassing than being caught in an agonized moan, it was sitting on the gym floor staring up at a cocky recruit. Involuntarily, her eyes ran up his body, and she felt herself faltering. He was still in trunks and shirtless. Not that she hadn't seen male recruits this way before, hundreds of them, but none from this angle exactly. Was that what made him seem so physically imposing? Or was it the memory of what she'd seen him do out there on the field?

"Need a hand, *what*?" she repeated.

"Need a hand . . . to get up?"

He was playing innocent, but she knew damn well it was an act. "Need a hand, *ma'am*," she snapped.

He held out his hand, and she batted it away. "I'll get up when I'm ready." *And when I can do it without falling on my nose,* she thought.

"So . . . can we talk?" he pressed.

She pushed to her feet and stood facing him unsteadily. It hadn't escaped her for a moment that he still hadn't complied. "Sure, we'll talk," she said quietly, "just as soon as you get it right, Raphaell."

"Hell, this *is* the lunch hour," he pointed out. "Couldn't we dispense with the—"

Kate swacked dust off her shorts and knees. "I don't care if it's the cocktail hour. We're not dispensing with anything. When you address me you observe the rules, Raphaell. If I show up in your *dreams*, you snap to attention and you say *yes, ma'am*." She squared her shoulders, determined that he show her the proper respect. She was not just another woman! She was his D.I. "Am I making myself clear, recruit?"

His green eyes sparked with anger, and she answered him with a few sparks of her own. If he wanted a showdown, he was going to get one.

"Crystal clear," he said, adding the word *ma'am* under his breath.

"Good, then what was it you wanted to talk about?"

"This morning, the workout—" Exhaling, he raked a hand through his hair and let the words hang as though stopped by his own sense of frustration. He said nothing for the next few moments, just stared at her darkly, and gradually the anger in his eyes banked and became something else, something complex that Kate couldn't read. Or was afraid to read. She felt his curiosity, his sharpened interest and realized that his scrutiny was far more threatening to her than his anger.

"I don't like being anybody's whipping boy," he said quietly. "Not even yours."

She breathed in, her heart quickening. "You think I'm singling you out?"

"Yes." He was staring at her, silent again, and it felt like a contest to see which of them would turn away first.

"What is it, Raphaell?" she asked at last.

He smiled faintly. "I was thinking about what would happen if you showed up in my dreams."

"Raphaell—"

"Sorry... couldn't help myself."

Kate's head arched up. "You'd better watch that kind of talk, recruit." She crossed her arms, her breath high in her throat. "It could get you into a lot of trouble."

Smoky lashes lowered, a breathtaking contrast to the flash of curiosity in his green eyes. "Yeah?" he said. "What kind of trouble?"

Kate's pulse quickened. For a split second she was mesmerized by his eyes, by their indecipherable signals, just as she had been at the first inspection. But this time she reacted with a quick flash of heat. "It could get you tossed out of here. How's that for trouble?"

"Really?" His eyes narrowed. "And who'd do the tossing?"

Did he think she was bluffing? He hadn't done anything serious enough to get himself thrown out yet, and being a lawyer, it was possible he knew that. Still, she told herself, this incident was a start. She kept her voice level, but firm. "Keep it up and *I'll* do the tossing, Raphaell. I'll throw you so far, you'll need a rickshaw to get back."

"A rickshaw?"

He was fighting a smile. Wishing she'd picked a tougher image than that of a man pulling a wicker wheelbarrow, Kate fought one, too. And lost. "Dammit, Raphaell," she said under her breath, shaking her head. "Wipe that grin off your face. *Attention!*"

His head snapped up and his eyes locked forward.

"You're going to write Essays of Understanding until the cows come home for this one, Raphaell. I want one on respecting your superior officers, one on attitude and one on breach of conduct. All of them addressed to the executive training adviser. Do you *hear me*, recruit?''

"Loud and clear, *ma'am*."

"Good, then we understand each other. At ease."

He relaxed, his eyes flicking to her. "What did I do?" he said, an edge to his voice. "Forget to brush? My deodorant? Why have you got it in for me?''

"I haven't got it in for you. This isn't personal—" She broke off, caught by the look in his eyes and the emotional waver in her voice. Suddenly she realized what she'd been fighting and denying all along. This *was* personal, very personal. Even now there was an electric snap of attraction between them, and they both knew it—a connection that had nothing to do with the academy or with her being a D.I. and him being a recruit. Nothing to do with it, and *everything* to do with it.

She felt that silvery sensation in her stomach again, stronger now, deeper, the *ching* of sound. "I think you'd better get out of here, Raphaell," she ordered. "Go...*now*."

He shook his head slowly. "No way," he said, his voice low, sandpapery. "I'm calling you out, Sarge. If you want to have me thrown out for breach of conduct, now's your chance, because I'm not going anywhere until we get a couple of things straightened out."

Kate stared into his green eyes and felt herself being drawn into every D.I.'s nightmare. The instructors relied on discipline, psychology and peer pressure to keep the recruits in line. With a rebellious recruit only the last had any effect at all, and that was negligible. It was a funny thing about power, Kate had learned. To work, it required the cooperation of the powerless. Most recruits never caught on to that. Rebels were born knowing it.

Raphaell's behavior told her he knew all about power games—and that only gave her one choice.

"Eyes, *front*, recruit! Now, listen to me and listen good! We're not straightening anything out. This is the *end* of our conversation. Do I make myself clear?"

"Yes—"

"Yes, *what*?"

"Yes, ma'am."

"If you want to talk to me in the future, you make an appointment and you come to my office. *Never* approach me this way again." Without waiting for his reply, she took two steps back from him, made a neat left-face and headed for the door. When she reached it, she remembered the essays. Without turning back, she said, "Have those essays on my desk by tomorrow, all of them."

She took hold of the doorknob and twisted, but her hand slipped on the unyielding metal. She tried it again, twisting harder. The knob wouldn't give. The door was locked? *Locked?* Whirling, she pressed her back against the door. "What have you done?"

He stared at her a moment, shook his head. "Nothing."

"Who locked this door?"

"I don't know," he said, starting toward her, "but I wish I'd thought of it."

"Stay where you are." She caught hold of the doorknob again, wrenching it, panic darting in her belly. "*Stay where you are*, Raphaell. That's an order."

"What in the hell do you think I'm going to do?"

"I don't know...but someone locked this door. And you had reason."

He hesitated, folding his arms slowly and evaluating her in the casual, loose-hipped style she associated with cockiness. His eyes brushed over her, vibrantly green, and then he nodded, as though he'd come to a decision. "What the hell," he said, exhaling, "I've broken so many rules already, one more isn't going to matter."

"*Raphaell—*"

Kate's emotions ran riot as he strode toward her. She tensed, pressing back against the door, bringing her hand up as he halted in front of her. "Whatever you've got in mind, Raphaell, don't do it. Not if you want to stay in this program."

"I had the feeling you wanted me out of the program."

"Maybe I do, but not this way."

Their eyes met and held and Kate felt as though she was going to suffocate, her heart was pounding so hard. It wasn't a physical threat she feared. She knew how to respond to that. This was something else...confusing, dizzying.

"What is it you think I'm going to do?"

The question was sincere, but she had no answer for it.

He moved in closer and propped a hand on the door alongside her head, gazing down at her, waiting for her answer, that shimmer of electricity in his eyes. The lashes that had mesmerized her before were dusky and beautiful, but they didn't soften his eyes. They made them stunningly erotic. An errant thought flashed through Kate's mind, mesmerizing and terrifying. These were the eyes of a slow and sensual lover, a man who could make a woman die from pleasure before he was through with her.

"I don't know *what* you're going to do," she said faintly, "but I *am* sure of one thing. If you had anything to do with this door being locked, it's going to get you thrown out of here."

He leaned toward her and she felt a clutching sensation in her stomach. Deep muscles pulled quick and tight, and her heart flared with a strange sweetness as he bent toward her. "Raphaell, God, *don't*—"

"Don't what?" he said.

A second flashed by, and then without warning, he gave the door a sharp push with his hand. As it creaked and popped open, he smiled and stepped back, still staring at her. "Well, I'm glad we got that straightened out," he said. "The door was jammed."

Chapter Four

Tilted back in her chair, Kate gazed out her office window at the workout yard. It was late afternoon and the area was deserted except for one or two recruits running laps around the quarter-mile track. She'd just finished her paperwork for that day, including an incident report of the confrontation in the gymnasium with Raphaell.

She tapped a finger on the chair's wooden arm, her Irish temper still simmering. Attitude problems like Raphaell's were difficult to document and even more difficult to prove. Still, she was going to have to take it up with Art Buchanan, the executive training adviser.

She drummed the wood with her fingers and a faintly bemused smile softened her expression as she thought about the jammed door. Damn showboater. Must've thought he was real cute gazing into her eyes with one hand propped on the door above her head. *Well, I'm glad we got that straightened out.*

"Ma'am?"

The question jarred Kate out of her reverie. She turned and saw Raphaell standing in the doorway. He was at attention and in full uniform, regulation all the way, including his required navy blue headgear.

"Permission to enter, ma'am?"

Kate sat up warily. Was this some kind of a stunt? Her heart felt uncomfortably light in her chest. "Come in, Raphaell," she said, standing.

He marched in, snapped a right-face and came to attention in front of her desk. He was so damn military, Kate had to fight the impulse to salute him. "Something on your mind, Raphaell?"

"Yes, ma'am. The essays, ma'am. I'd like to submit them now—*with* your permission, ma'am."

"Three ma'am's in one breath? That's loading it on a little, don't you think, Raphaell?"

"Ma'am?"

Kate watched like a hawk for any trace of a smile lurking in his angular features. "The essays aren't due until tomorrow," she reminded him, finding it impossible not to notice how trim and high-gloss he was in uniform. He looked like some shiny homecoming hero.

"You're right, ma'am," he said. "I'll come back tomorrow." He took a step back from her desk. "Permission to leave?"

"At ease, Raphaell." Kate could usually tell when she was being put on, but she caught no inflection of amusement in his voice, no flickering of a smile on his lips. His eyes might have given him away, but they were hidden beneath the headgear's visor. "I'll take the essays now."

"Yes, ma'am." He stepped forward, handed them to her. "I hope they're satisfactory."

Kate read through the first short essay quickly and skimmed the other two. Satisfactory? They were immaculate—neatly hand printed, perfectly formatted, succinctly worded. The content conveyed just the right touch of comprehension and contrition. He'd even managed to work some sincerity in between the lines. Kate had graded hundreds of essays in her time, but these were a D.I.'s dream. If he was trying to make the point that he could follow orders, he'd made it. Eloquently.

"Are they, ma'am? Satisfactory?" he added as she lifted her head.

"Yes..." she said. "They seem to be." She stared at him, questions filtering through her mind that she couldn't put words to. Mostly she was baffled by his inconsistent behavior. She hadn't a clue what he was up to, or even if he was up to anything. "You realize these essays don't stop here, Raphaell. I'll be submitting copies to the executive training adviser, who, if he deems it appropriate, will refer them to the dean."

"I understand that, ma'am."

"You do...?"

It was his next question that made Kate realize she was still gazing at him, brows furrowed.

"Am I dismissed, ma'am?" he asked.

"Oh...yes."

As he disappeared through her door, she sat slowly, her eyes on the empty doorway. Some moments later, propping an elbow on the desk, she tapped her lower lip thoughtfully.

"So...which is he?" she murmured finally, giving voice to her thoughts. "A D.I.'s nightmare? Or a D.I.'s dream?"

Kate took a sip of the milk she'd warmed and wrinkled her nose in distaste. If you disliked milk in the first place, warming it only added to the yuck factor, she decided. She set the mug down on the night table next to her bed, sighed, picked it up again and took another swallow. Her mother had forced her to drink warm milk in her childhood when she couldn't sleep and it had worked then. Of course, her mother had always laced the stuff with Irish whiskey....

Unfortunately, Kate didn't have any whiskey, and she had to report for work the next day. Think of the calcium, she told herself, holding her breath and finishing off the contents of the mug. She shuddered, settled back into the pillows and picked up where she'd left off with a late-night talk show on television. The guest was a clairvoyant who read breakfast toast crumbs and laundry lint.

Listening to the bearded man predict triumphs and disasters on a worldwide scale, Kate wondered if her own cinnamon raisin bagel crumbs had foreshadowed disaster that morning. *Beware of strange men in gymnasiums*, they'd probably spelled out just before she'd carelessly swept them into the disposal.

Closing her eyes, she reflected on Ty Raphaell, shirtless in the gymnasium, on Ty Raphaell in full uniform in her office, on dreams and nightmares. In the privacy of her own apartment, the sanctuary of her own bedroom, she could allow herself the dangerous luxury of thinking about him... and about the dreams *she'd* been having.

They'd begun the first week of class, startling little flashes that had slipped into her normal sleep cycle. One night she'd dreamed about opening a shower door in the women's locker room and finding Raphaell inside. Two nights later, she'd dreamed about being abducted during a warm-up run and dragged into the bushes by a shadowy man who looked like the troublesome recruit. She'd awakened bathed in sweat and shouting "Eyes *front*, Raphaell!" Just today, she was sure he'd locked her in the gymnasium. And she'd been *wide-awake*.

Kate's thoughts darted irresistibly back to the moment when he'd defied her orders in the gymnasium. *What the hell*, he'd said, striding across the room toward her, *I've broken so many rules already, one more's not going to matter*. Recalling vividly how he'd halted in front of her, Kate realized she was fingering the buttons of her silk nightshirt. Her heart rate was up a little, too. "This is not good, Madigan," she murmured, pressing her fingers to the pulse at her wrist. "Ninety-eight beats a minute? A resting pulse? Not good at all."

She turned her attention back to the talk show and the psychic. Shaking her head at the absurdity of it all, Kate switched off the TV, but there was no real mirth behind her smile. Nights were difficult. Alone with her thoughts, no struggling recruits to distract her, no reports to file, she came face-to-face with Kate Madigan—a woman whose needs she didn't completely understand.

Especially now. She couldn't remember ever having thoughts and dreams that tugged at her so uncontrollably before. They twisted her neat little world out of shape and left her feeling at emotional odds with herself. Rolling to her side, nestling into the pillow, she made up her mind that she wasn't going to let herself dwell on Ty Raphaell anymore, certainly not on the way his eyes made her feel...or the way he'd touched her that night in the bar...*or whether he would ever touch her again*.

Those kinds of thoughts were too dangerous, too seductively powerful. They brought a sudden tenderness to her throat. They made her feel things that were poignant and beautiful, yearnings she'd cut herself off from years before. And they threatened to erode the one thing she'd always been able to count on—her own steely willpower.

All her life Kate had set her sights on what she wanted and gone after it. Her grit and tenacity reflected her staunch Irish upbringing. The Madigans were a passionate people, but conspicuously practical in the channeling of those passions. They controlled their feelings and their destinies, always. It was what Kate knew, it was the way she lived and had always lived.

And though she hadn't yet realized it, it was exactly that kind of single-mindedness that was bringing her up short now. She truly didn't understand what was different with Raphaell. It frustrated her that she couldn't deal with him the way she did everything else. Efficiently, effectively. It baffled her that she hadn't been able to set aside her awkward and inappropriate feelings for him and get on with the business of training recruits.

It wasn't the sexual element of the attraction that confounded her. She'd felt all those things before...for Glenn, her fiancé. Not with the same intensity, perhaps, or sense of the forbidden. Glenn hadn't been one of her recruits. He'd been a policeman, too, and loving him had never interfered with her work or her goals. He'd enhanced her life, made it complete. Everything was the way it was supposed to be, the way she'd been told it would be—and should be for two people in love. No surprises in their relationship, no dark secrets to test their happiness. They were as enduring as the Santa Monica hills. And then he'd been killed....

A cord tightened in Kate's neck. Seconds later, she saw a flash of red behind her right eye and felt a dull stab of pain. Rolling onto her back, she closed her eyes and resigned herself to the incipient headache. She knew by now that the physical pain kept her from sinking into emotional quicksand, and she wanted that protection tonight. She didn't want to think about Glenn...or remember. The abrupt and tragic loss of her fiancé still triggered unresolved conflicts in her, even after six years. She handled it by not allowing herself to dwell on the past—ever, if she could help it—and by making the future all-important.

A short time later, as the headache subsided a little, Kate leaned over, turned off the light and let the room's quiet soothe her. Aware of her own breathing in the darkness, she assured herself that her reaction to Raphaell was a temporary aberration. It happened all the time in reverse—recruits developing crushes on the D.I.s. Given the fact that Raphaell was older and deadly attractive—the kind of man she would have found appealing under almost any other circumstances—her responses to him weren't that surprising.

She just needed a little time to do some emotional housecleaning, to bring her thinking into line. "A little 'reassessment' time," she murmured, "and I'll be fine."

On that thought she fell asleep... and drifted deep and dreamlessly. It was only as morning approached, in the still hours just before dawn, that the disturbing reveries stole into her unconsciousness again...

Steam was billowing from the shower stall as Kate walked up to the door. She discerned the shape of a man through the frosted glass, heard the water beating against his body. Touching the glass, she made a clear spot with her fingertips and gasped softly at the jet spray pummeling the magnificent male form. Colliding forces. Her throat drew tight and her heart was a craziness inside her as she let her own towel drop and pulled open the door....

"Raphaell?"

Steam enveloped her, a hot and sultry cumulus cloud that walled her off. His name echoed like a shout in a canyon, growing gradually more faint, disappearing.

"All you need is some time," a man's voice said.

"Raphaell, is that you?"

She gasped as a hand took hers and drew her into the churning, turbulent water....

All you need is time.

Suddenly lights blinked on, dazzling klieg lights high in the rafters. She was in a gymnasium and Raphaell was striding across the floor toward her, stripping off his T-shirt, letting it drag on the floor for several strides before he dropped it.

"Stop where you are, Raphaell! That's an order!"

"Time, Kate," he murmured, *next to her, leaning over her, his hand propped against the door. "Time is all you need, and it's the only thing I can't give you. I need you now."*

"Raphaell, I can't.*"*

"Why do they call you Storm?" he asked. *"Show me why they call you Storm."*

Kate felt the world go dark and swirl away as he leaned into her, breathtakingly close, his hands at her throat, stroking her like a warm breeze, magically undoing the buttons of her nightshirt.

Why do they call you Storm?

"A storm is a disturbance of the elements of nature," a faraway voice was saying. *"Lightning, thunder, a violent commotion."*

"That's what I want, Kate," he said against her hair, *"to get lost in that storm, that violent commotion. I want to feel all that exquisite fire and fight around me."*

Kate gasped as he slipped his hand inside her nightshirt and cupped her breast. *"Tell me about the commotion inside you, Storm,"* he said, his breath hot in her hair. *"Tell me about it now."*

His bare skin against her flesh brought Kate the most exquisite sensations she'd ever known. It felt as though light was bursting everywhere he touched her. His fingers sank into her wantonly, possessively, and sent streams of pleasure rioting through her.

There was no mistaking the intention in his gaze. His green eyes pierced right through her body. He was going to make love to her, and the erotic beauty of his mouth reminded her of the premonition she'd had about him...that he would be slow and sensual, that she would die of pleasure before he was through with her. *"This can't be hap-*

pening," she told him, a throaty moan in her voice. "I'm dreaming you, Ty Raphaell. I'm dreaming this."

"Yes, you're dreaming." His lips parted slightly, half smile, half kiss as his mouth touched down on hers with a pressure so light it was nearly unbearable. He lingered there, a dragonfly, exciting her senses, tantalizing her nerves. Briefly, too briefly.

Sliding her nightshirt off one shoulder, he pressed his lips to her ear. "So let's dream some more," he said. "Come on, Storm, let's bring the night down around us."

His tongue feathered the lobe of her ear, dipped inside, shockingly intimate. His hands were on her body, thrilling her sweetly, hotly, and her nightshirt was sliding down her skin. "Yes," she said, dreamily astonished at her own nakedness and suddenly awash in urgent desire. "Yes, yes..."

And then, just as he drew her down to the floor, a voice cried, "No!"

Kate bolted awake, clutching at her pillow and breathing in deep, rhythmic gulps of air. It took her several seconds to get her bearings. "That was a dream, Madigan," she rasped, reassuring herself. "It was *only* a dream."

Switching on the light, she threw back the covers and shot out of bed, pacing, thinking. "Lord, but *what* a dream."

Moments later, she dropped to the floor and began counting out push-ups. Her muscles, especially tender from the workout the day before, screamed at her. When she hit thirty, she hollered back at them and sank to the floor. "It's always darkest just before it goes black," she gasped, remembering the advice she gave her recruits when they complained.

Kate was in her office grading the radio code tests the next afternoon when Melissa MacGregor knocked on the partially opened door.

"Permission to enter, ma'am?"

"Come on in, MacGregor," Kate said, glad to see the young recruit. "Sit down."

MacGregor sat stiffly, her pale gray eyes apprehensive.

"At ease, MacGregor," Kate said, smiling to relax the recruit. "I make it a policy *not* to follow the Procedures Manual in here, so please ... make yourself comfortable." Kate settled back in her chair, wondering what was going on with the rookie. She looked intense, to say the least. "What's on your mind?"

MacGregor drew in a breath. "I just want you to know that I'm dead serious about this program, Sergeant Madigan. I'm *going* to graduate."

"I hope you do, MacGregor."

"Do you really?" MacGregor sat forward, her voice tight, her hands clasped.

"Is something wrong?" Kate asked.

"Sergeant Haggerty doesn't think I can make it," MacGregor blurted. "He's been calling me the runt of the litter. Says I need a body transplant. Says I'm all brain, no brawn."

MacGregor blinked, her eyes bright, and Kate knew she was fighting back tears. "I think he's trying to pressure me into quitting," she said, her voice cracking.

The rookie looked down at her hands, distraught, and Kate quelled a sigh. Now she understood why MacGregor was so uptight. "Terrible Tommy" had struck again. Kate had asked him to take the workout session for her that morning. Her excuse was a touch of the flu, but the truth was she hadn't felt up to dealing with Raphaell.

Staring at MacGregor, Kate made a decision. It was possible that Tommy was right about this recruit, but if he wasn't, then MacGregor deserved a chance to prove herself. And he was *wrong* about me, Kate reminded herself. Bless his hard-boiled heart, her co-worker still didn't understand a basic truth about the majority of the female species. Once they made up their minds, damn little deterred them. It was part of their biological inheritance, Kate suspected, part of that instinct that made them fight to the death for their young, if necessary. Women were a tenacious breed, but Tommy hadn't figured that out yet. He thought because they cried they were weak. Poor Tommy.

MacGregor looked up and Kate smiled. "I'm going to tell you a little secret," Kate said, "but don't let it go past this office. Runt of the litter is a compliment compared to what Sergeant Haggerty used to bellow at me when I was one of his recruits."

"You had Haggerty?"

Kate nodded and watched MacGregor's eyes spark with hope. "You survived him? How did you do it?"

"Blood, sweat, a few tears—but *never* in front of him. He respects a fighter, MacGregor. Don't give up, no matter what he throws at you. And don't ever let on that you're afraid of him. He's mostly bluster," Kate added softly, wryly. "We all are. We don't want anybody to wash out, MacGregor. But it's our job to find out who can take the pressure and who can't." She glanced out the window, looked back at the recruit. "I think you can take it, MacGregor."

"Yeah?" MacGregor's voice cracked and she consulted her hands. "Yeah," she said at last, looking up, smiling. "I think I can, too."

Kate's chest tightened. The earnestness in MacGregor's expression was eerily reminiscent. This was a kid who would jump the Grand Canyon blindfolded if that's what it took to make the grade. She remembered going through the recruit's file the same night she'd gone through Raphaell's. MacGregor had been classified an underachiever in high school, which hadn't surprised Kate since the file also noted the recruit had grown up in a series of foster homes.

"The academy is pretty important to you, isn't it?" Kate asked.

"It's everything," MacGregor said matter-of-factly. "A person's got to be good at something in life, and this is it for me. This is what I want."

"Police work? Why?"

"I want to wear the blue uniform, the gold badge. I want to prove to myself that I can do it."

Kate felt a moment of concern. That had always been a large part of her motivation, too, proving she could do it, but was that the right motivation? Was that enough? "It's not about uniforms and badges, MacGregor. It's not a glamorous job."

"I know," MacGregor agreed, sobering. "It's about earning the *right* to wear the badge. And once you've done that, well, you know what they say—" she shrugged, as though a little embarrassed at the emotion in her voice "—then you can make a difference."

"Even if it's just helping little old ladies across the street?" Kate pressed. "Traffic detail?"

"Sure," MacGregor said, laughing. "After this place, traffic detail sounds like a slice of heaven to me." She looked at her hands again and the laughter became a compressed smile, full of emotion and youthful optimism. "I'll take traffic detail, I'll take it all, gladly. But I'm going to be a detective someday, Sergeant Madigan, a detective."

"A detective?" The words slipped out under Kate's breath. She'd wanted that once, too. Before she'd met Glenn. She was going to specialize in fraud. She'd even had supplemental college courses planned in business and contract law. It wasn't as though Glenn hadn't supported her when she'd told him, it was just that he'd wanted something so different. His dream was to be a D.I. And then when he'd died so suddenly, everything had changed—

Kate looked up, saw the young recruit staring at her and wondered how long she'd been lost in thought. "I hope you get what you want, MacGregor," she said, turning again to look out the office's one window. "I hope you get it all."

"Thanks," MacGregor said.

Kate nodded automatically, but her thoughts had already drifted again. She rose slowly and walked to the window, staring out at the workout yard where several recruits were running the obstacle course. She was thinking about her time out there ten years before. She was thinking about the pain, the triumphs, the challenges. Watching, smiling over the roughness in her throat, she wondered exactly what it was she'd wanted then. Ten years ago. And what she wanted now.

Kate wasn't sure how long it took her to realize that Raphaell was among the recruits in the yard, but when she finally discerned his dark hair, his straining features from among the others, she felt a jolt of recognition. It disrupted her breathing for a second, made her blink. He was negotiating the obstacle course's seven-foot wall, scaling it like a rock climber attacking a sheer cliff.

"He's really something, isn't he?" MacGregor murmured.

"What?" Kate hadn't even realized the rookie was next to her.

"Raphaell," MacGregor said, unqualified admiration in her voice. "The guy's a major force."

"What makes you think I was looking at Raphaell?"

"Oh," the rookie laughed softly, "I didn't. *I* was looking at him . . . and talking to myself mostly. Sorry, ma'am." MacGregor's eyes widened, curious. "Were you?"

"Was I what?"

"Looking at Raphaell?"

Kate felt herself coloring. *Looking at him, dreaming about him, losing my grip on reality because of him, that's all,* she thought. "Yes, I was looking at him," she admitted drily. "He's rather difficult to miss, isn't he?"

"Impossible to miss," MacGregor agreed, returning her gaze to the window.

"Like the bad apple in a barrel," Kate muttered.

"Like a proud panther in a platoon of house cats," MacGregor countered with a soft breath. "Gosh, look at those triceps, those *pecs*. Wanna bet he eats Wheaties like the big boys do?"

Kate considered the rookie askance. "Maybe you'd better take a few laps around the track, MacGregor, and burn off some of that energy."

"Yes, ma'am." MacGregor smiled, blushing. She saluted smartly and headed for the door. Almost as quickly as she disappeared through it, her head bobbed back into sight. "Thanks for the advice," she said. "I'm going to make the grade, ma'am. You just watch me."

"I'll do that, MacGregor."

As Kate turned back to the window, she noticed that Raphaell was standing alone now, apart from the other rookies. He was too far away for her to see his expression, but there was no missing the fact that he was staring in her direction, looking directly at her, in fact, unless she was mistaken. He seemed poised in decision, about to walk her way.

Her senses quickened as the dream flashed through her mind. *Why do they call you Storm?* Staring back at him, she had the oddest sensation of being unable to turn away. For a second, she felt pinned to the floor, frozen in a picture frame. *A violent commotion,* a muted voice was saying.

Kate blinked, and her vision blurred for an instant. Through the mist, she thought she saw Raphaell break his hesitation. Was he coming her way? Grabbing for the venetian blind rod, she twisted the blinds shut. Moments later, huddling in the dim confines of her office, staring at the shuttered window, she realized how ridiculous all of this was. She couldn't hide indefinitely. She had to face him sometime.

A sharp rap on the door brought her around.

"Come in," she blurted automatically.

The door creaked open and Art Buchanan, her supervisor, peered in. "Madigan? Why the hell's it so dark in here?" he said, fumbling for the light switch.

The light popped on and Kate blinked and brushed at her uniform.

"You look like a cornered rat, Madigan," he boomed, his fleshy, reddened features furrowing skeptically. "What have you been doing in here?"

Kate stared at her executive training adviser, the man whose blood pressure had topped out, according to rumor—and whose job she'd applied for. "Uh...meditating, sir?" she said tentatively. "It's great for clearing the mind. And for lowering the blood pressure," she added, hoping that was true. "Ever tried it?"

His grimace said she'd picked the wrong alibi.

"I don't have time for catnaps, Madigan. I've got an academy to run. Think you can stay awake long enough to talk to me about one of your recruits?"

"That shouldn't be a problem, sir. Which one?"

"Ty Raphaell."

Kate experienced a moment of confusion. She hadn't expected her problem with Raphaell to come to Art's attention so quickly. She hadn't even given him the essays yet. Had Raphaell gotten himself into trouble somehow, with one of the other D.I.s or instructors? That possibility shouldn't have surprised her, but it did. She hadn't seen him as an overt troublemaker. In fact, she'd thought the problem was confined to her personal difficulties with him, which made the situation that much harder to explain. What had he done? she wondered.

"You listening, Madigan?" Buchanan barked. "I said that young man's shaping up to be one of the best recruits we've ever had!"

Chapter Five

Shaping up, sir?" Kate was virtually certain she hadn't heard him right. "Raphaell?"

Buchanan nodded, oblivious to Kate's perplexity. "I've been watching him, Madigan, keeping an eye on his progress, if you will. Of course, it's early yet in the term, and anything can happen. A dark horse could pull up from the back of the pack, but barring that, I think he's O.R. material."

Outstanding recruit material? Kate tried not to look astonished. That award was for meritorious achievement. It was given to the recruit who graduated from the academy with the most points accumulated in both academics and the physical fitness modules. She'd won it in her class! *She'd* been the dark horse. "O.R., sir? Are you sure?"

Buchanan looked puzzled. "Why not O.R.? He's a damn saber-toothed tiger out there on the obstacle course, and Tommy tells me he's leading the class academically. He seems to be outstanding in every respect."

Now Kate's astonishment was complete. Only the irony of the situation kept her from gasping. A moment ago Raphaell was a proud, prowling panther, and now he's a saber-toothed tiger? she marveled. Throw in a ringmaster, and you had a circus act! "It's true Raphaell excels in those respects," she protested, "but he's . . . an attitude problem."

"How's that? An attitude problem?"

Kate indicated the stack of files on her desk. "There are already three Essays of Understanding in his file." Prepare yourself, Madigan, she thought, if he wants to know the circumstances that precipitated those essays, you're going to have some explaining to do. *Well, sir, I thought he was going to ravish me in the gymnasium, but it turned out all he was doing was popping a jammed door.*

"Attitude, well, that's different," Buchanan said. "Let me see his file."

Kate fished it off the top of the stack and handed it to him. "Breach of conduct, sir," she said. "He was ordered to address me as *ma'am*—several times—and he didn't comply."

"I see," Buchanan said, perusing the essays.

Kate wet her lips expectantly.

Moments later Buchanan slapped the file down on the desk and looked up at her. "This boy can write his way around an essay, Madigan. I'm impressed. I'd say he's done a damn fine job of acquitting himself, wouldn't you?"

Raphaell, you were born under a lucky star. "I found the essays . . . satisfactory."

"Don't be modest, Madigan. This is as fine an example of our disciplinary process in action as I've seen. I just hope you can whip the rest of your rookies into shape before the white glove inspection."

"I think I can, sir."

"I hope so, Madigan. The dean plans to be there."

Kate's throat went dry. "The dean . . . ?"

Buchanan winked at her. "Off the record?"

Kate nodded.

"Put on a hell of a show," he advised. "Light up that Grinder and you could be the next Art Buchanan. Catch my drift?"

"I do, sir."

"'Course the job nearly killed me. You know that, don't you? Blood pressure as screamin' high as a treed cat."

"I heard, sir."

He spun on his heel and strode for the door, halting as he swung it open. "Oh, and Madigan... About that recruit of yours, Raphaell? I think *one* memo would have done it, don't you? Discipline's fine, but we don't want to be over-zealous now, do we?"

"Uh...no, sir."

"Handle him right, Madigan, and that strapping young man should do you proud. Make a fine class sergeant for the inspection, don't you think?"

"Sir?"

"Lights out, Madigan?" He tapped the light switch—a little joke about her meditating, apparently—whisked out the door and slammed it behind him, leaving Kate staring after him, her eyes narrowed in disbelief. If she'd tracked that conversation correctly, Ty Raphaell was now her star recruit! The O.R. award? Class sergeant? The whole damn academy seemed to want to make a hero out of him. Was she the only one who saw him as a problem?

He is a problem, she thought, walking slowly to the shuttered window. He's insubordinate, he doesn't accord me the proper respect, *he makes love to me with his eyes*. Only she couldn't very well say that to Art Buchanan, could she? It was her attraction to Raphaell, and her inability to handle it, that was complicating everything.

She reached for the venetian blind rod and hesitated. It had always been her style to attack problems, to hit them head-on, but that strategy wasn't working for her now. She felt a tug of frustration, and then, strangely, in its aftermath, a momentary quietness, a calm spot in the midst of her confusion that brought with it a glimmer of insight. Maybe she was fighting too hard, like the fish struggling against the hook and embedding it deeper? Perhaps if she could relax a little, resist the feelings less, they would pass.

An alien notion to be sure, but keeping it in mind, Kate took a deep breath and released it slowly. She drew the blinds open, half expecting Raphaell to be standing on the other side of the window. Through the sudden glare of sunlight, she discerned that he was still out on the field, almost exactly where she'd first seen him, only now he seemed completely absorbed in stretching exercises. Resting one leg on a wooden bench, he leaned forward over it in a hamstring stretch.

A warm sensation ran along Kate's skin, faint, but strong enough to prickle the downy golden hair on her arms. Reality seemed to elude her for a moment. Had she imagined him staring at her earlier, walking toward her?

Fascinated, continuing to watch him, she tried to relax and go with the feelings stirring inside her. He was bent over his outstretched leg, and muscles seemed to surge down his thighs and up his back. He was power in repose, a study in dynamic tension. But *had* he started toward her or had she been daydreaming?

She remembered reading somewhere that dreams were supposed to be unconscious wish fulfillment. If that was true, then what were daydreams? she wondered. The next step toward fulfilling that wish? And of course she knew what followed daydreams—*fantasies*.

"Kate Madigan doesn't have fantasies," she vowed softly, firmly, yanking the blinds closed as Raphaell stretched and bent over to touch his toes. "They're not covered in the Policy and Procedures Manual."

Out in the workout yard, Ty saw the blinds blink shut again. Smiling, he drew up one vertebrae at a time to a standing position, did a couple of quick neck rolls and began a slow jog to the men's locker room. His thighs and calves were tight as piano wire, and he was looking forward to a long, hot shower.

He hit the locker room door just as the last of the recruits tumbled out.

"Coming over to the cafeteria?" one of them yelled.

"Buffalo chips au gratin again," another chortled.

Ty laughed and waved them on. Actually, he was glad to have the place to himself. He wanted to be alone with his thoughts.

Moments later, soaping himself down in a steaming shower, he felt the tension begin to ease from his muscles. Pacific Police Academy, he thought, massaging a knot in his shoulder. The place may kill me yet. He bent, rubbed a kink out of his thigh muscle. And if it doesn't, *she* will. What were they calling her now? The Screamin' Blue Meanie? As he recalled, that's what some fast-thinking recruit had baptized their beautiful, baleful D.I. in her absence that morning.

Turning, letting the hot spray pummel his back, Ty mused on some of the other choice names the platoon had come up with for Sergeant Madigan. She didn't know about their irreverent games, of course. Not that she would have minded, he suspected. Kate Madigan was a tough lady, and she didn't seem to care who knew it.

He'd asked himself several times if that was what he found so compelling about her. He knew most men would have been threatened by all that feminine power, maybe even turned off. She represented something unassailable, and unattainable. But then nothing had ever come easy to Ty Raphaell, unattainable women included. He liked it that way.

He also suspected that it was what he sensed *under* the toughness that really compelled him. What was all that armor protecting? Was she the kind of woman who held it all in, and then unraveled with a touch? He'd had his share of fantasies about what she would be like at that moment when her impulses took over, when her body dominated her head. Yes, he realized, that was what compelled him, that vision of touching her, of having her sigh and cry out and come apart in his arms.

His gut muscles tightened on a stirring emptiness. Turning, he faced the water again, letting the sharp spray needle his body. I want that, he thought, riveted by the hollow sensation inside him, by the sudden, sweet awareness of his own need. I want *her*... that way.

Later, toweling off the streaming water, he reminded himself that he could jeopardize his own study if he got involved with her. A relationship with a drill instructor could strain his credibility as a researcher. Still, he felt compelled to take that risk.

It came to him as he pulled his clothes out of the locker that he'd made a tactical error in pursuing her here at the academy. She couldn't let down in this environment. She couldn't forget who she was. If he was going to get anywhere with Kate Madigan he had to make her forget she was *Sergeant* Madigan.

It would take time, patience and a new strategy.

That was okay. He had all three.

With the white glove inspection just a few weeks away, Kate knew she had miracles to accomplish if the platoon was going to be ready. She set an unrelenting pace for her troops, drilling them until they marched like a Marine Corps honor guard, grilling them until they knew the Procedures Manual and the California criminal codes forward, backward and sideways. She'd never put more energy into a class of recruits. "You guys are going to *shine*," she vowed, buffing them up when their spirits flagged. Through it all, she praised and persecuted, and finally, her enthusiasm was so infectious that her rookies actually began to dream of hitting the heights she'd set for them.

"This isn't because of the promotion, Tommy," she would insist automatically whenever her coinstructor regarded her askance. "You know I'd be riding their behinds whether I was up for E.T.A. or not." In her heart she believed it. She'd always demanded perfection from her recruits, and this class was no different. But in private moments when it all caught up to her, when she felt the exhaustion, too, she questioned her own motives. She *did* want Art Buchanan's job, and she did want to prove to herself that she could keep Raphaell in line. Yes, those needs were influencing her, but *not*, she told herself, beyond the bounds of appropriate drill instructordom.

Still, every now and then during the weeks of rigorous preparation one of those calm moments would return, and she would wonder if, perhaps, her driving ambitions were also a way of keeping certain urges at bay. She told herself the urges were nothing, hormonal fluctuations, but in fact they were stirring little shocks of sexual longing that came at unexpected moments, like the precursors of an earthquake, and had nothing to do with promotions or keeping recruits in line. She tried to ignore them, and managed—for the most part.

To Kate's great surprise and relief, her star recruit had been behaving himself in recent weeks, too. Raphaell seemed to be responding to her efforts right along with the other cadets—or at least he was putting on a good show of it. There'd been no more incidents in bars or gymnasiums, and Kate was grateful for that. He'd been quiet and respectful, even distant at times, and all the while excelling at everything he did. If he kept it up, she realized, he might well be the O.R. Occasionally, she'd noticed him studying her, or thought she had. She was never quite sure whether she'd seen it—or fantasized it.

Melissa MacGregor was coming along, too, though Kate was still defending her to Tommy. He was openly concerned about the young woman's inability to handle the body drag, a strength exercise every recruit had to master before graduation. Kate had been about to give MacGregor a few insider's tips one afternoon when she'd seen Raphaell coaching her. Kate had backed off and watched with silent admiration. It was always better to let the recruits inform and inspire each other. They would need to be able to count on each other in the line of duty.

Of course, there were the usual glitches as the weeks passed, the minor setbacks that every new class encountered, but all in all, Kate was quite pleased with how things were going. Her professional life, it seemed, was once again on track.

Kate's good fortune held until something unexpected happened in the last two weeks before the inspection. *The dreams came back*. At first they were shocking and disorienting replays of the gymnasium encounter, with Raphaell coming toward her, relentless, and Kate waking up with a cry on her lips, unable to stop him any other way. The morning after a night of such dreams, she was shaky and nervous for hours.

Eventually, though, they began to take on a different mood...secret, shadowed and beautiful. There was always a candlelit darkness, a man and woman languidly defined by the flickering flames. Gradually she would realize that the woman was her, the man, Raphaell, that it was just the two of them hidden away from the world.

Egyptian green under their dark veil of lashes, his eyes would hold her spellbound, caressing her, drawing up sensations from within her that were almost unbearable. Silent eyes. Hungry eyes. He was making love to her with his gaze, slowly, explicitly, never touching her, *forbidden to touch her*, and yet arousing her until she gasped with pleasure and trembled with surprise. And finally, when she couldn't stand it any longer, when her heart and her limbs and even her bones ached for contact, she would reach out for him...and lose him to wakefulness.

Always she came out of these dreams with his name on her lips and filled with longings that brought pain to her breathing and tears to her eyes. And always with the same question in her mind...*does he dream about me?*

Kate stared down her extended right arm at the paper target hanging some twenty-five yards away. The barrel of the .45-caliber automatic she held gave off a dull metallic shimmer in the fluorescent lighting of the academy's indoor firing range.

She sighted the paper figure of a man with her strong eye and concentrated on bringing the rhythms of her breathing under control, lowering her heart rate. Ignoring the circle on the figure's chest area that indicated the heart, she targeted the head instead. She was going for a tight shot this time—right between the eyes. At last, when she was ready, elbow locked, senses totally honed in on the focal point, she squeezed the trigger.

The muted crack of sound hit her ears and the recoil jerked her arm up almost simultaneously. "Gotcha," she breathed, straining against the weapon's kick. It jolted up her arm to her shoulder, a shock wave her nervous system compensated for automatically. Instantly she riveted her eyes back on the target, brought her arm steady, and she was ready again, the weapon sighted to fire.

She didn't take the second shot. In fact, the gun's ammo magazine was empty, but it was part of her training to re-sight quickly, to be ready to fire immediately in case she ever needed to.

"Let's see how you did, Ace," she murmured to herself, pulling off her sound suppressors, the protective headgear the academy required. She hit a switch on the wall behind her that backlit the target, squinted down the alley and smiled. Bingo! "Right between the eyes."

Moments later, packing up her gear, she reflected on the confidence she felt in this small firing range. Here, at least, she called the shots. She liked the necessity for total concentration, total control. She actually enjoyed the shock to her equilibrium, the sense of mastery when she righted herself. She seemed naturally to be good at things that required swift and sure action.

Smiling, she thought about the fiercely competitive dart tournament she and Tommy had going at Mother's. They were at ten games each now, but they'd decided their next match would be for the whole shebang, the Dart Championship of the Free World. Darts she could handle, she thought ironically. It was the rest of her life that had her reeling, her inner world, the emotional tangles, the confusing conflicts.

She was leaving the firing range when she saw one of those conflicts walking toward her. It was a sunny Saturday morning, and like herself, Ty Raphaell was dressed in civvies, a white raglan sleeve sweater, jeans and leather moccasins. His dark hair looked like it had been carelessly hand combed, and the effect was all very low-key... and stunning, Kate admitted reluctantly.

"I'd like to request a counseling session," he said, reaching her. He added, "ma'am" almost as an afterthought.

"I can see you on Monday, my office, before class," Kate informed him crisply, moving around him to leave.

He shifted position, very subtly, very casually, but in effect he was blocking her path. "I was hoping we could talk today."

"Today?" She studied the nuances hidden in his expression, and the thought that flashed through her mind was *not a chance*. He would be dangerous at any speed today.

"Shouldn't take long," he said.

She studied her watch, stalling, and found herself unable—or was it unwilling?—to come up with even the flimsiest of excuses. "All right, then . . . I'm not doing anything at the moment."

"Great," he said, smiling at her.

They walked across the campus to her office, and just by the fact of their proximity, Kate felt as though she was breaking every rule ever set down. It was the dreams, she supposed, the daydreams, the errant thoughts running through her mind even now as she and Raphaell walked side by side. It was *guilt*. I haven't done anything wrong, she defended silently.

Problem was, she realized all at once, she *wanted* to do something wrong. The insight hit her like an unexpected, low voltage shock. Kate Madigan wanted to break the rules, run in the rain, walk on the grass. She wanted to be bad for once, *just once*. And if a woman was going to be bad, she thought, glancing over at Raphaell's long-legged stride, *this was the man to do it with*.

Unsettled by the turn her thoughts had taken, Kate picked up the pace. Soon they were walking briskly, silently, the tension between them as high-pitched as a dog whistle. By the time they reached her small office, her breath was coming fast, and she had a sensation of lightness in her chest. She breezed through the open door, walked to her desk, turned and faced him. "What is it you want, Raphaell?"

He seemed a little disconcerted by her directness. Or maybe it was the quiver in her voice. "I'm out of breath," she said and then flushed. Don't do this, Madigan, she warned herself. Don't turn this counseling session into another high school date!

"I noticed you were spending a lot of time at the firing range," he said, taking the chair she indicated. "Actually, I'd heard you were a crack shot, and I'm having a little trouble with the proper . . . stance."

"Your stance?" Why don't I believe that? Kate thought.

"I've been blowing my point-shoulder shots from the twenty-five yard line. Any ideas what I might be doing wrong?"

He was talking about the exact shot that Kate had been practicing at the range. She'd never observed Raphaell at the firing line—the academy had special instructors for the marksmanship training—but she couldn't imagine him having much trouble mastering the stance or anything else. Still, he'd asked, and it was her job to provide answers. "The position is pretty basic, Raphaell. Face the target, extend your arm and sight down it. The trick is to concentrate and relax at the same time. Slow your breathing, lower your heart rate. Don't tighten up, and don't anticipate the recoil, or you'll blow the shot."

He nodded, settled back in the chair as though he planned to stay for a while. "They say you're good."

"Good?"

"I heard you've picked up some marksmanship awards."

"Oh, yes, a couple."

"Then you'd have to be good."

He smiled, and Kate found herself smiling with him, and relaxing a little. "Is that what you came here for?" she asked. "To talk about marksmanship and my medals?"

He nodded. "That . . . and curiosity. I wanted to get another look at this legendary office. Rumor has it you have trophies on the wall, the heads of failed rookies."

Laughing, she swiveled in the chair from side to side, indicating the walls with her outswept hand. "It's not true. Have a look."

"I knew it wouldn't be."

"You did?"

His green eyes flashed a brilliant yes. "You're tough, but only on the outside."

"You're sure of that?" Kate knew this conversation was veering toward the personal, but she made no immediate attempt to straighten its course. She was feeling good today, captain of her ship, so to speak, and it had been so long since she'd spoken with him, other than to shout orders. Besides, she liked the odd way her heart was beating, the *on edge* feeling he gave her.

"I'm not sure of anything about you," he said, gazing at her. "Call it a hunch."

"Call it a lucky guess," she murmured. She liked being gazed at, too.

Their eyes connected for a minute, and Kate knew something unequivocally. She *did* want to break the rules and run in the rain. *With him.* The thought frightened her, but she allowed it through—and the sharp whoosh of pleasure that came with it. Women were always talking about the man of their dreams. She was staring at hers.

Does he dream about me?

"Been to Mother's lately?" he asked.

She nodded.

"What's the attraction?" he asked. "Not Slam, I presume."

"Slam?" She didn't connect at first. "Slam, no—I guess he's found a new hangout. I haven't seen him around Mother's since you—" She shrugged, letting him fill in the blanks. "Actually, Tommy and I are in the final throes of a dart tournament. We're on for Championship of the Free World tomorrow night."

"Really? Tomorrow night?"

She sighed. Well, you did it, Kate Madigan, she thought. You just did it. You practically invited this man to join you at Mother's. "Raphaell, I think it would be better if you didn't—"

"Didn't what?" he cut in, sitting forward.

His gaze brushed over her features and hesitated on her mouth, so intently Kate felt her lips tingle.

"Ease your mind," he said at last. "I have no plans to storm Mother's on my white steed. I got the message last time. You can take care of yourself."

"Thanks," she said, aware that the inflection in her voice was faintly disappointed. "It's nothing personal. It's just that the administration frowns on—"

"Fraternization. I've heard." He pushed the sleeves of his sweater up above his elbows and looked out the window. "Recruits and brass don't mingle. Well," he said, pushing out of the chair and standing up. "Thanks for the target practice tips. I'm sure I'll shoot straighter from now on."

Kate didn't want him to go. She'd never felt a stronger impulse in her life than the need to say something to make him stay. She stood up as he walked to the door. "Raphaell?"

He turned back to her.

She touched the top of her desk with her fingertips, and then she shrugged. "At the range? Don't pull the trigger, squeeze it ... gently."

They stood there, staring at each other, unable or unwilling to say what was really on their minds, and finally Kate gave in to the impulse to question him about something that had been bombarding her for weeks. "Why did you come here, Raphaell?" she asked. "What do you want from me?"

Her breath caught as he closed the door and leaned against it, staring at her.

"What do I want from you?" he said. "It's not very complicated. One of these days, you and I are going to be together and there won't be any uniforms or badges between us. That's all I want, Kate Madigan, that day."

Kate was still standing there, staring at the door long after he'd closed it behind him.

Chapter Six

A country rock ballad throbbed from the old nickel-odeon-style jukebox at Mother's bar, and a half dozen couples swayed on the sawdust-strewed dance floor. At the other end of the dark, hazy establishment, in the only brightly lit area, a fast and furious dart game was in progress. Tommy Haggerty moved off to the side, his last shot taken. Now it was Kate's turn. A crowd of onlookers milled around her as she brought up her hand, the dart positioned delicately in her fingers.

"Watch out, folks," Tommy muttered. "She's got a wild arm."

Kate broke concentration just long enough to give Tommy a wicked grin. "Good try, Haggerty," she said, "but not good enough. This one's mine."

"Blast him off the map, Sarge," a barmaid called.

Kate brought the dart back until it was aligned with her right eye and took aim. She'd started with 301 points, the standard number, and subtracted each score progressively, the object being to get the score down to exactly zero. Any lower and she went bust, which Tommy had just done. With fifty points on the board and just one dart left, Kate *had* to hit a bull's-eye to win.

Imagining the trajectory of the dart in her mind, she saw it hit the target. Tommy was sitting on the railing that sectioned off the area, and by his slow, sidelong stare, it was fairly obvious that he didn't think she could do it. Smiling, she drew in a breath. His skepticism was just the incentive she needed. If she hit, she took the game *and* the title. The Dart Championship of the Free World was hers.

A hush went up as she refocused and, with a quick flick of her wrist, sent the feathered missile flying. It flashed through the air and penetrated the board with a soft, satisfying thunk.

"Bull's-eye!" someone yelled.

"Bull's-eye?" Kate punched the air and whooped. Within seconds the cheering crowd had closed in on her and lifted her onto their shoulders. Bounced and jolted around the room, she managed a wobbly wave at Tommy.

"Lucky shot," he called out.

"You should be so lucky," she called back. Laughing, she gave him a thumbs-down. "Oops!" she cried as she was boosted from one pair of shoulders to another. "You're going to drop me, you lunatics!"

"Let's throw her!" someone yelled.

"No way!" Kate scrambled helplessly to get down but only entangled herself more. Tossed in a sea of anonymous hands, she was flipped onto her back, dropped into a cradle of arms and tossed into the murky air of Mother's like a buttermilk pancake.

"Put me *down*!" she demanded, plummeting back into the human safety net, landing half in, half out, her feet brushing the sawdust floor.

"Again!" the cry went up. "Heave!"

"No! Help!" she pleaded, grabbing the first hand that was thrust her way. Laughing and scrambling to get her footing, she was tugged free of the commotion.

"Sorry!" she gasped, tumbling into the masculine body attached to the hand. "Thanks...*Raphaell*?" She reared back, staring up at the charismatic smile of her star recruit. "Raphaell, you—"

"I know," he said, urging her away from the protesting crowd, "you can take care of yourself."

Kate caught her breath and shook her head. "No, actually, I was going to thank you for saving my life."

He laughed softly, surprised. "I guess you never know when you're going to need a guy on a white horse."

Straightening her clothing, Kate was about to ask him what he and his horse happened to be doing at Mother's when she saw Tommy coming their way. Ty noticed him, too, and drew up, affecting a stance of attention.

"Relax, Raphaell," Tommy said gruffly, cuffing him on the arm. "Good catch, by the way. I thought they were going for a moon launch."

"Speaking of which, why didn't *you* save me?" Kate asked.

"I'm a sore loser." He winked at her and turned to Raphaell. "You any good at darts? I've got to whip somebody's butt before I go home tonight."

"I'm lousy," Ty said.

"Great, let's play."

Kate sat at the bar and nursed a beer while the two men battled it out. They traded quips and insults like a couple of beer-drinking buddies, and the rowdy bar crowd loved every minute of it. Raphaell was the better player, Kate saw immediately, sensing that he was holding back so as not to embarrass Tommy. She wasn't sure it was possible to embarrass Tommy, but she appreciated the gesture on Raphaell's part.

As the game progressed Kate's thoughts turned to more immediate concerns. The very fact that Raphaell was here meant he had to have something in mind, and it was probably inappropriate. After their conversation in her office, she hadn't known what to expect from him. *Someday you and I are going to be together, and there won't be any uniforms or badges between us.* Surely he didn't think that someday was tonight?

Kate glanced down at herself and lost a heartbeat. Her snug jeans and green silk blouse weren't a uniform by any stretch. She considered Raphaell again and decided he looked positively dangerous in his faded denims and biker's leather jacket. It's all right, she told herself, Tommy's here. Raphaell would have to be crazy to make a move with Haggerty around.

That thought didn't comfort Kate as much as it should have. It reminded her that somewhere along the line she'd lost faith in her own ability to handle Raphaell. And it brought home a deeper truth. She wasn't at all sure she *wanted* to handle him.

The cheering drew Kate's attention back to the dart game. Raphaell was the underdog and everyone wanted him to take the game. When he did, with his last three darts, the place went wild.

"Lucky shot," Ty said, laughing, shrugging as he turned to Tommy. He'd taken the words right out of the D.I.'s mouth. "Is this going to cost me on the Grinder tomorrow?"

"Tomorrow and the rest of your recruit life," Tommy muttered good-naturedly.

Kate smiled consolingly at Tommy as the two men joined her at the bar. "Not your night, Haggerty."

"How about you?" Ty asked her. "Is it your night?"

Kate exchanged glances with him, and a crackle of something quick and electric passed between them. "It has been so far," she said.

"He's looking to get even for all those push-ups," Tommy said, chuckling. "Go on, Storm. Shellac his fanny for the academy."

"Are we talking about darts?" Kate asked.

Ty grinned at her. "You man enough . . . ma'am?"

Kate stared at the challenge hidden in his green eyes. She'd seen it once before, the first night of class. *Take me on for size, lady cop.* Instantly she felt her competitive nature stirring. He was good, that she'd seen. But she was better, *that she knew.* "Okay, Raphaell," she said, sliding off the bar stool, "let's do it."

They left Tommy at the bar ordering a beer, and walked to the wall of dart boards.

"What are we playing for?" he asked, as she picked out the three darts she would use for her first turn.

"The thrill of victory?" she said under her breath, staring at the board, focusing in, honing the concentration that had won her medals.

"How about a dance?"

"Dance?" She followed his eye to the couples clinging to each other on the sawdust floor across the room. "You mean like that? Slow dancing?" Her stomach went hollow at the thought.

He picked up his own darts, considered the board intently. "Sure. I'll even let you lead."

Kate was shaking her head as he glanced over at her and laughed softly, his smile slow, irresistible. "What's wrong, Sarge? Afraid you can't take me?"

"I can take you, hotshot," she said. "I could take you tied up and blindfolded. I just hope you're prepared for a week's latrine duty when you lose."

He studied the darts in his hand, nodding, traces of the smile still on his lips. "You're on."

Their first game was tense and tight. They went for triples all the way, bringing their scores down quickly—until they both went bust and had to start over. It was in the second game when Ty pulled off a Hat Trick, three bull's-eyes in a row, that Kate realized the extent to which he'd been holding back with Tommy. He wasn't good, he was terrific.

She played valiantly from that point, hitting every shot she tried, including three triple-twenties in a single turn, and then, to the anguish of the crowd, she went bust by five points on her last throw.

Kate joined the crowd of spectators. She was out of the running, but she hadn't lost the bet yet. Ty still had to bring *his* score down to exactly zero for an official win.

The tension spiked as he took his turn. A groan went up as his first dart, a wild throw, left him with a Madhouse— three points remaining on the board.

"If he pulls this off, he's a magician," Tommy said at Kate's shoulder.

Kate didn't respond. The Madhouse was a mythmaker, a near impossible shot. To make it, Ty had to hit a one, followed by a double one. Tight with nerves, she watched him pick off the first point he needed. The onlookers roared their approval.

Perspiration glittered on Ty's forehead as he prepared for his last throw. He brought the dart up, flush with his right temple and held it suspended. Kate counted the seconds until, with a soundless flick of his wrist, he sent it flying. She didn't want to look, but she was mesmerized as the silver bullet zinged through space. A gasp went up and she quickly averted her eyes. *He'd done it.*

"Did he make it?" someone cried.

A hush fell over the room.

"Looks like he hit wire," the scorekeeper said, walking over to investigate.

He *hadn't* done it? Kate looked up.

The spectators swarmed toward the board while Raphaell remained at the firing line. At last the scorekeeper turned back, grinning. He gave Raphaell a thumbs-up and the noise nearly took the roof off.

By the time the crowd settled down and Raphaell reached Kate and Tommy at the bar, Kate had herself in hand. "Lucky shot?" she asked wryly.

Ty's gaze lingered on her, penetrating the cool barrier of her defenses. "I guess this is my night, too," he said.

"I hope so, son," Tommy cut in, thumping Ty on the back, "'cause now you're going to have *two* D.I.s on your case tomorrow." He finished off his beer, nodded to Kate. "I think we ought to clear out of this place before he humiliates the academy any further. How about it? You ready to go?"

"Sure," Kate said instantly.

"You're leaving?"

It was Ty who asked the question, and as Kate looked up at him, she saw the veiled surprise in his expression. If she left, she would be running out on their bet and they both knew it.

"Get a hustle on," Tommy told Kate, "I'll walk you to your car."

Kate broke away from Ty's questioning gaze, her heart quickening. Finally she shook her head. "No, that's okay, Tommy. You go ahead. I've got a bet to honor." She turned to the D.I., flushing slightly.

Sharp-eyed, he scrutinized Raphaell. "If you've got a rematch in mind, Kate, watch yourself. This young man's hot tonight."

"No kidding," Kate said faintly, "but somebody's got to defend the academy's honor."

"Yeah . . . well, *adios*." He looked them both over again, took a step back and swung around to leave. "Bring the cup home," he called back to Kate over his shoulder.

She watched him push through the door and knew he hadn't been fooled. Tommy had figured out what was going on, she was sure of it.

"I'm up for a rematch if you are."

Ty's voice came from behind her and it was quietly sincere, as though he'd sensed her conflict.

"I'll even front you a few points," he said, smiling as she turned to him.

"I don't need charity, Raphaell." With mock brusqueness, she added, "You got lucky tonight, that's all."

"That I did." He glanced at the dance floor where couples were stuck to each other like taffy wrappers, swaying ecstatically to "How About Us?," a slow, dreamy ballad for new lovers. His smile relaxing, he stared into her eyes. "They're playing our song."

Kate shoved her hands into the pockets of her jeans and lifted a shoulder. "You mentioned a rematch?"

"Rematch?" He laughed softly. "Sure, but the stakes would be higher. Instead of dancing, I'd probably want to—"

"Never mind. Let's dance."

She started for the dance floor, walking ahead of him, unaccountably nervous, her thoughts centered on how she looked and whether she had any lipstick on. Why do I always revert to adolescence when I'm around him? she wondered. She was self-conscious and short of breath. She actually wanted to ditch him and hide in the girl's room!

Stopping at the edge of the dance floor, she thought about the academy's no-fraternization policy. Even to mention it now would look like a cowardly attempt to back out. Especially since there was no one at Mother's who remotely cared whether they were fraternizing or not.

"Maybe you ought to turn around?" Ty suggested, his breath rustling her hair.

Kate nodded, but she didn't turn. The last thing she would have called herself—or permitted anyone else to call her—was a coward. In her street duty days, she'd dealt with armed and dangerous criminals. Why was this simple encounter with a man on a dance floor so difficult?

She felt his hand at her waist, and a slow thrill spread up her spine. It hit her all at once that she was frightened, and this was a different kind of fear than she'd faced on the streets. It was vague and centered deep in her vitals. It was intimate and somehow paralyzing.

"Hey, what's wrong?" he said.

"I'm not sure we should do this."

"It's just a dance." His voice lulled her with its husky resonances. "One dance."

"I know." How did she explain to him that it had been a very, very long time for her? She'd already imagined what it would be like dancing with him, and she knew when he took her in his arms, that some part of her, some tiny, vital wall of resistance would melt. Everything would be different then. The protective barriers would be gone, and she would feel things she shouldn't feel, want things she shouldn't want. What if she couldn't come back from that? Tomorrow she had to be his D.I. again. Tomorrow, she had to be tough.

She turned to him, her heart pounding. "I can't do this," she said.

His features clouded, but he gave her no argument. "Okay," he said quietly, "I'll walk you to your car."

She was fine until he took hold of her hand, *fine until he touched her*. The heat of his flesh, the firm grip of his fingers sent a little shock of longing through her. "Wait," she said, pulling back, shaking her head, unable to look at him.

"Kate...?"

She couldn't catch her breath for a minute. She couldn't think for the crescendo of nerves inside her. "Hold me," she whispered finally. "Just hold me."

He tugged her to him easily, gently, and took her into his arms, his fingers slipping into the hair at the nape of her neck.

Her body's reaction was strange and beautiful. A soft gasp spread through her, tangling in her throat. It didn't matter that he held her effortlessly, that their bodies were barely touching, she felt as though she was drowning in the nearness of him. The caressing heat of his hand on her skin, in her hair, sent paralyzing currents of electricity down her spine. All of his movements were slow and unhurried, but to her rushing senses, the contact felt sudden and exquisitely physical.

"Oh God, Raphael!..."

His hand slowed, stopped. Neither of them moved until she looked up at him.

"What is it?" He searched her features with certainty now, as though he could see through all her defenses and read every secret in her heart. "What are you frightened of? I just want to hold you. I'm not going to hurt you."

A kind of pain welled in her throat and she closed her eyes, averting her head. "You're already hurting me," she whispered, her heart tightening. How did he know he could hurt her? And why did she feel so fragile, so exposed? It was as though he, and only he, could touch the vulnerable places deep within her, open old wounds with his eyes, his words.

He enfolded her closer, rocked her gently. "Dance with me," he whispered into her hair, "one dance. Whatever that hurt is, let me take it away for a little while."

Music swirled around them, a love song with poignant lyrics about star-crossed lovers and second chances. The sweetly reminiscent chords brought a tenderness to Kate's chest.

Her breath seemed to stop as Ty took her hand, slipped his fingers through hers and drew her up against him. A sigh escaped from her throat as they began to move to the music. Closing her eyes, she entwined an arm around his neck and felt him shudder at the contact. The awareness that he was vulnerable, too, filled her with a strange, sweet flare of pleasure. As the music swelled around them, she clung to him, swayed with him, mesmerized by the way their bodies touched and by the sharpness of her responses. The simple artistry of their movements pulled at her senses, drawing her attention to the curve of his shoulder beneath her fingers, to the layered muscles of his back and especially to his hands as he guided her around the floor. They were strong and sure, his hands... *all a woman needed*.

She'd nearly forgotten what it was like to dance with a man, to be held this way. "*Please,*" she said, murmuring the word into the soft leather of his jacket, "hold me tighter." She gasped as the sudden strength of his arms crushed her breasts softly against his chest and brought their thighs into contact. Racked with a sweet jab of desire, she drew her head back, swallowed hard and felt him kiss her throat.

"I knew you'd be soft here," he said, his lips making love, slowly, sensually, to her flushed skin.

The moment she'd predicted had come. The barriers of resistance were melting, her very bones were melting. She'd missed this terribly, missed being touched and embraced by a man, being *loved* by a man. The dreams, the little shocks of physical longing she'd had since meeting Ty had all warned her that this would happen... this beautiful liquid heat. It streamed to every nerve center in her body with a force that left her breathless. Needs? Wants? Yes, she needed these riveting sensations. Yes, she wanted this glorious inner fire.

Gradually she realized they had stopped moving except for their slow swaying to the beat of the song. He'd locked both of his arms around her, and one of his hands had drifted to the base of her spine. The heat of his fingers pressing into the softness so near her buttocks sent tingly shocks of pleasure through her.

"Raphaell..."

"Shh," he hushed her, "don't stop the music yet." He worked his other hand deeper into her abundant hair, cupping the back of her head and coaxing her to nestle into the hollow that formed his shoulder. She softened against him, closing her eyes, listening to the heavy thud of his heart with rapt absorption.

Irresistibly then, she pulled back to look up at him and felt her stomach seize up in a knot. Desire darkened his eyes, and the promise of sensual pleasure in his mouth was breathtaking.

"Such stormy eyes," he said, feathering her eyelashes with his fingers. As he drew those same fingers along her cheekbone and traced the contours of her face, Kate's intuition told her they were going to kiss... and if they did, they would never stop.

The realization was thrilling and terrifying. She averted her eyes.

"Hey... what did I do?" he asked, laughing softly. "Come back, look at me."

She did finally, shaking her head, feeling foolish.

He smiled a little, his eyes shimmering, but he didn't bend to kiss her. It was as though he knew it, too. *Once they started, they would never be able to stop.* "Trust me," he said, pressing his lips to her temple, "just for a little while longer. Don't leave me yet."

They began to dance again, and when the song finally stopped, Kate didn't want it to be over. She wanted to stay in his arms, dreamy warm, pressed up against the muscular heat of him. She wanted this to be a high school date so that they could hold each other all night, no rules, no barriers, only fiery passion and sweet promises. She wanted to run and laugh and be kissed in the rain.

He brushed his lips against her forehead and pulled back to look into her eyes. "Well . . . what's the verdict? Does it hurt anymore?"

"No," she said, laughing. It didn't.

"Want to talk about it?" His hand was resting on her throat, his thumb tracing her jaw. "I'd sure like to know what makes those eyes so stormy and sad."

It welled up in her suddenly, the urge to tell him about her past, about lost hopes and shattered dreams, about her own fears of loving and losing again—and just as suddenly she realized how risky that was. It would open up memories, trigger emotions she couldn't deal with.

"Sorry, I'm going to plead the fifth," she said, stepping back, out of his arms. She drew her hand from his and as their fingers lost contact, it felt like some magic spell had been broken. Kate felt alone and adrift. Suddenly the bar seemed noisy and stuffy again, the music too loud.

"One beer for the road?" he asked.

"No, I don't think so," she said, wishing desperately that she could stay, that she had never let go of his hand. "I probably ought to go. You, too . . . there's class tomorrow."

A glance passed between them, a quick look galvanized by a tiny lightning bolt of understanding. They both saw it, the truth in each other's eyes. They wanted to be together.

"Come on," he said, catching her hand and pulling her toward a back exit. He pushed through the door to a narrow alley lined with trash cans.

It was dark in the alley, a little chilly and the air was pungent with the odor of onions and fried hamburgers from the greasy spoon next door. Kate felt a shiver of illicit excitement. Still holding his hand, she leaned against the exit door and smiled. "Sneaking out the back door into the alley? This *is* like a high school date."

"High school date?" He looked intrigued. "That's a great idea. It brings back an adolescent fantasy of mine. I always did want to kiss the teacher." He propped his hand on the door above her head, gazing down at her in much the same way he had in the gymnasium.

Kate felt a warm languor wash over her, and the sensation was overwhelming. It felt as though she was being dragged down into the shimmering depths of his green eyes, into a drowning pool of sensation. "Raphaell ... don't ..."

Wry laughter crinkled his eyes. *"Don't?"* he breathed. "Who says I was going to? Maybe this door is jammed." He gave it a push and Kate felt it click into position and lock behind her.

"I guess we're stuck out here," he said. "What do you think we ought to do?"

"Call for help?"

"Help," he murmured huskily, leaning toward her.

She lifted her face to him and tilted her head, anticipating the sensuality, the softness of his mouth. As his warm breath touched her lips, her heart surged, a craziness inside her, just like in her dreams.

He didn't kiss her immediately. Instead, he aroused her with his mouth, coaxing her lips open with his tongue, whispering unintelligible secrets to her senses. Their only other contact was his hand warming her waist, and as he drew it up slowly toward her breast, telling her how soft she was, how beautiful, Kate felt a painful surge of anticipation.

Her stomach muscles tensed, and her skin flushed with fire. "Don't touch me there," she pleaded, but the moan in her voice gave her away.

"Where?" he asked, running his thumb along the sensitive underswell of her breast. "Here?"

"Yes." She arched up as his hand cupped her, his fingers pressing into her flesh. The flash of desire in his eyes was

staggering, and a harsh breath caught in his throat. But still he didn't kiss her. "God, it's incredible," he said, gazing down at her, "the way your heart is racing beneath my fingers."

Bombarded by sensations, Kate reached up to pull his hand away. She couldn't let him do this, couldn't let him talk to her and touch her this way.

"Don't stop me," he whispered, massaging her breast sensually, gently with his fingers. "I want to touch you this way everywhere. All those secret places that are soft and warm, even softer than this."

Her heart rocketed as he leaned into her and fitted his mouth to hers, drenching her with all the slow, sweet pressure she'd dreamed about. Excitement soared, scrambling her senses. She felt beautiful and exquisitely weak. She felt naked and bewildered as a lost child, a part of her crying out to be held, loved.

"Raphaell," she murmured in her throat. She was pressed back against the door, her head tilted up by the possessive heat of his kiss. He caressed her breast, feeding deep, aching pleasure to her senses. She was stunned by the sensations, dizzy, drugged... but it wasn't enough. She wanted to be closer. She wanted to be in his arms.

She touched his hand, and as he pulled back, she dragged in a breath, trembling. "Hold me," she pleaded, moaning as he gathered her into his arms and kissed her thoroughly and passionately, pulling her away from the door, turning with her in his arms.

In the crazy heat of the moment, she opened her mouth to him, and he plunged his tongue into her sweetness, exploring the warmth, the moist depths. He took possession of her with a swift passion that sent Kate's blood searching through her veins. Was this what he would be like if they were in bed—hot-blooded and urgent? Or would he be the slow, sensual lover of her dreams? As he slid his hands down to her buttocks and brought her up against him, she knew he would be both.

And she knew something else. He was aroused, fully and frighteningly aroused.

He broke the kiss. "I want to take you home with me, teacher, now, *tonight*."

"Home?" She pressed her hands against his chest, dazed, momentarily confused. "Tonight?" A tremor of surprise crept into her voice as she realized what he meant. "I can't—" Still dizzy from the roar of blood in her head, she breathed, "I can't go home with you, Raphaell. You must know that's impossible."

"Impossible? Why?" He rubbed her arms, warming her as she shuddered. "We danced," he said. "We just kissed. Nothing's impossible anymore."

Kate's heart tightened, wrenching inside her. She barely knew how to explain it to him, and yet the reasons were so fundamental. How could he not know? "I thought you understood, Raphaell. *Please* understand. We shouldn't have done this. We *can't* do it again. I'm a D.I. There are rules."

He released her, turned away, swung back. "Hell, I understand about the rules, but no one has to know we're seeing each other."

Shivering in the night air, Kate caught hold of her arms. Suddenly it was cold, so cold. "Raphaell, *listen* to me," she said, desperate to make him understand. "If I continued to see you, I'd be jeopardizing my job, my badge. And you'd be jeopardizing your recruit status. They'd suspend us both."

All at once, the dank cold and the squalor of the alley caught up with her, and the revulsion she felt spilled over onto what they'd just done. "Even if they didn't catch us," she said, "I couldn't sneak around like that." She turned away from him, a sick feeling in her stomach. She must have been crazy to think she could get away with this. You didn't play on the freeway and not get hit. It was her fault, not his. She was the one in authority. She was the one who wore a badge, who'd been entrusted with a solemn duty to discharge.

"I'm sorry," he said at her back. "It happened, that's all. I got carried away. I guess we both did. Let me walk you to your car."

She shook her head. "No," she said, the D.I. authority edging back into her voice, "go back into Mother's, please. I want to be alone. I *have* to be alone."

"Alone? In this alley?"

"Raphaell, I'm a cop, dammit. I'll get to my car all right, but I'm not going into that bar again. Now, *please,*" she said, her voice catching emotionally, "*get the hell out of here.*"

Chapter Seven

Kate awoke from a restless, dream-tossed night with a throbbing pain in her temples. Even to open her eyes brought anguish. It was another headache, of course, but it wasn't about the two beers she'd had at Mother's or the troubled night. It was about guilt.

Rolling onto her side, she opened one eye, slowly, and winced at the glare of light from the window. She knew how easy it would be to lay the blame for last night's craziness on Raphaell, or on human nature, for that matter. She'd been ambushed by emotional needs—and by a man who read those needs, understood them and spoke to them so eloquently. What woman *could* resist him?

But Kate couldn't let herself off that easily. It wasn't just that she'd sidestepped the rules. What was infinitely worse, in her own mind, was that she had breached her own personal code of ethics. She'd lost control of the situation and her own emotions. What good was a D.I. who gave in willy-nilly to her own impulses and passions? How could she expect to control a rowdy bunch of recruits if she couldn't control herself?

Nothing like last night had ever happened before, and the whole messy episode was inexcusable in Kate's book. "You are the lowest of the low, Madigan," she said, gingerly rolling to the edge of the bed and sitting up. "Slug slime, that's what you are."

Her mood sank even further after she'd called in sick. "It's a headache, Art, not a brain tumor. I don't need the paramedics," she'd insisted, persuading the executive training adviser that a couple of aspirin and some bed rest were the best course of treatment for her condition.

Later that morning, lying on her unmade bed and staring out the window, she thought about Art's reaction. His surprise was perfectly understandable. She hadn't missed a day of work since she started with the academy five years before. She'd even shown up for an inspection once with walking pneumonia. No wonder he'd assumed she was dying.

Unaccountably, it was missing work, more than anything else that felt like the ultimate indictment of her professionalism. If success came in threes, she wondered, then what about failure? She'd already logged two of them—a necking session with a recruit and a blight on her perfect attendance record. What was next? she wondered. Or maybe failure came in fours or fives. Maybe she had several more disasters to look forward to?

Moments later, in the kitchen, chewing on dry rye toast to curb her queasiness, she grappled with the significance of what she'd done. Yes, she had acted rashly and unwisely, but she hadn't done anything illegal, immoral or fattening. She wasn't going to jail. This *wasn't* the end of the world.

That rationale eased her conscience some, but it had precious little effect on her headache. Dropping toast crusts into the disposal, she glanced out the window and noticed the sun breaking through the haze. Another gorgeous day, she mused, depressed at the thought. She even felt out of sync with the weather.

Her headache had subsided to a dull throb over her right eye by the time she shambled into the living room and sank into the big, saggy leather chair that fronted her terrace window. Her apartment faced the pool, so she watched mothers playing with toddlers and a dozen or so other sunbathers enjoying themselves. Retirees and night-shifters, she supposed, wondering what other sort of people could afford the luxury of lolling around the pool, wasting an entire day. A wistful sigh escaped her lips. She couldn't remember when she had wasted an entire day—or even if she ever had. The idea of killing time, even an hour's worth, seemed so decadent to her, so contrary to the work ethic she'd been brought up with. *The Madigans are an industrious breed*, her grandpop used to announce at the dinner table. *They make time count*.

It struck her then that she'd been living in the apartment three years and she'd never once used the pool, never dozed alongside the water in the sunshine. Staring down at a plumpish woman lying on her stomach, her back shiny with suntan lotion, Kate seriously wondered whether she could ever relax and enjoy herself that way, letting life fend for itself while she lollygagged. On the heels of that insight, another surfaced. She *had* relaxed and enjoyed herself. Last night. And look what had happened!

She sat forward in the chair, her forehead pulsing. She had never crossed the line before last night, she realized, massaging her temples with her fingertips, never done anything she felt really ashamed of. Oh, maybe there'd been the time or two she'd exceeded the speed limit or neglected to mention the extra change a cashier had inadvertently given her. Her own mother had always said such mistakes were providence's way of righting the balance, that a cashier's error simply compensated for the times we'd unknowingly been shortchanged in the past or would be in the future. Mother's wisdom or not, Kate thought, it was a pretty flimsy rationale, and she'd suffered pangs the few times she'd used it. *Honest to a fault, the Madigans*, her grandpop used to say. What would he think of this mess? Kate wondered.

A shriek of childish laughter brought her attention back to the pool area. A father was playing with his young daughter, tossing her into the air and catching her as she splashed down. Something wistful welled in Kate's chest again as she watched. She didn't know why, but it made her sad to see such carefree joy—the children playing as though it was their inalienable right, the sunbathers chatting casually and sipping lazily from iced glasses. Even the lone swimmer doing laps disturbed her. It was all so alien to her experience. It made her feel alone and a little bereft.

Watching them, she couldn't help but wonder if she was missing out on something...some human connection as simple and basic as the capacity to have fun, perhaps? She wasn't sure *what* it was, but she knew it took a kind of freedom to enjoy yourself the way those people were doing, a freedom she must have lost touch with somewhere along the line. Or perhaps she'd never been free in that way. That thought disturbed her.

In her bedroom, moments later, she searched through dresser drawers and closet shelves wondering where she'd put the bathing suit purchased for a rafting trip she'd never quite gotten around to taking. She found the suit tucked under some cotton summer things that needed ironing. The flowered bikini was seriously out of style by today's daring standards, but that didn't concern her. She'd been wearing a uniform so long, she'd grown oblivious to fashion trends. Slipping out of her nightshirt to try the suit on, Kate realized she was already thinking of this as a challenge. It wasn't that she wanted to loll around in the sun so much as she wanted to find out if she was even capable of lolling...or just laughing and feeling like a child again.

The sun was blazing high in the sky as she walked out of her apartment door with a bath towel knotted around her hips.

Ty sat through the morning's classes on search and seizure techniques, his mind drifting constantly from the lecture. As the other recruits busily scribbled down notes, he stared at his notebook and the name he'd aimlessly been writing. He'd even doodled some thunderclouds and lightning bolts here and there around the edges of the paper. *You've got it bad, Raphaell*, he thought smiling.

He wrote the name again in bold, sensual strokes. *Storm*. And next to it he wrote a question. *Where is she?* According to the schedule, she was supposed to be teaching this morning's class, but Tommy had shown up in her place.

Ty had thought about nothing but Kate Madigan all night, dreamed about her and generally indulged in the kind of behavior he would have called obsessional in anyone else. He'd left her in the alley at Mother's only because she'd insisted. Afterward, he'd become concerned about her making it home safely, and he'd placed a call to the private investigator who'd worked for his law firm. Within twenty minutes, the man had called Ty back with Kate's home phone number and address. But Ty hadn't used the information. With Kate's training, the chances that she hadn't made it home were slight, and he had a pretty good idea how she would react to a check-up call at two in the morning.

It was her emotional state that Ty was concerned about. The force of her responses the night before had literally taken his breath away. The soft glint of pain in her eyes, the trapped, trembling desire in her body... and then the anger and remorse when she realized what she'd done. Kate Madigan had all the ticking intensity of a beautiful time bomb, he thought, pursing his lips—

Tommy Haggerty's bark sliced through Ty's thoughts.

"Okay, which of you knuckleheads knows the answer to that question?" the D.I. challenged. "How about you, Raphaell? You've been hanging on my every word, right?"

Ty looked up. "Sir?"

Tommy tapped his own head. "You need your bowling ball redrilled, recruit? Answer the question."

"Sorry, sir. What was...the question?"

"I asked you what a spiral search was."

Ty felt Melissa MacGregor poke him in the back. She was sitting right behind him and she was whispering something about starting from the center, but Ty couldn't quite hear what it was.

"You got an answer for me, son," Tommy pressed, "or is that a sealed vacuum between your ears?"

A spiral search? Racking his brain, Ty tried to recall if he'd read or heard about it in a prior lecture.

Tommy cleared his throat impatiently.

"I fail to recall the answer, sir," Ty said.

"Fail to recall?" Tommy snapped. "How the hell can you fail to recall something I talked about five minutes ago? What have you been doing all morning? Writing your memoirs? Let's see what you've got in that notebook."

"Just notes, sir," Ty said quickly as the D.I. strode toward him.

"Hold it, hold it." Tommy halted in front of Ty's desk and thrust out his hand. "Hand it over, hotshot. We don't want to deprive the rest of the class of your brilliance, now do we?"

Nervous laughter rustled around the room. *Damn,* Ty thought, holding up the notebook. He felt a flash of heat at the base of his neck as he watched the D.I. skim the name, the drawings.

Tommy's eyes narrowed and he lifted his head abruptly. Staring hard at Ty, he ripped the top sheet off the notepad and crumpled it in his hand. "I think you and I need to have a talk, recruit. See me in my office after class."

"Yes, sir."

The heat climbed Ty's neck. With the class gawking and grinning, he felt like a kid caught passing notes. The awkward moment brought home to him just how distracted he'd been by Kate Madigan. It also made him realize that his attraction to her ran a hell of a lot deeper than he'd realized or intended.

Ty forced his attention back to Tommy's lecture, but in a corner of his mind he was still speculating on Kate Madigan's whereabouts. Fortunately, he'd learned to concentrate on several things at once in law school, because as the class wore on, a third and even more immediate concern surfaced—the inquisition in Tommy's office.

When the moment came, Ty was unaccountably nervous for a grown man who'd stood before judges all the way up to the California Supreme Court. Facing Tommy Haggerty was as nerve-racking as his first visit to the principal's office in grade school when he'd pulled up Jenny Lafferty's dress and knew he was going to get the paddle for it.

Haggerty settled back into his chair, tapping his baton in his palm. "Who won the rematch?" he asked.

The rematch? "If you're referring to the dart game...uh, she did, sir."

"Smart move," Tommy said. "At ease, Raphaell. I'm not going to use you for target practice just yet. There are a couple of things I want to know first. Why don't you start with those lightning bolts you were drawing all over your notes—and that name, Storm. Explain all that to me, son."

Ty clasped his hands behind his back in the at-ease position. "Would you believe it if I said I'd always wanted to be a meteorologist, sir?"

The D.I. smothered a smile. "Is that your answer?"

"No, sir, it's not. The truth is I was wondering where Sergeant Madigan was this morning. I understand her nickname is Storm Trooper."

"And the lightning bolts?"

"I'm a nature lover, sir."

"A nature lover?" Haggerty rose from his chair. "Look at me, boy," he said, drilling Ty with his eyes. "Sergeant Madigan's whereabouts are the least of your concerns, is that clear? *Nature lover?*" He whacked the desk with his baton. "If you've got nature or *anything* else on your mind besides graduating this class, you get it *off* your mind. *Now.* You've already got three Essays of Understanding in your file, hotshot. If you want to go for four, you just keep up this goofball behavior. I'll give you four reprimands, I'll give you five, and then I'll escort your butt out that big front door myself. Am I getting through to you, Raphaell?"

"Yes, sir."

"Then get out of here, Raphaell. I'll expect to see you on the rifle range this afternoon."

Ty nodded. He had every intention of being on that rifle range this afternoon, but that was over an hour away. In the meantime, he had something else to do.

Ty spotted Kate as he was walking away from her apartment. He'd knocked several times on her door, but she hadn't answered, and since logic told him she had to be inside—the administration secretary had confirmed that Sergeant Madigan had called in sick—he'd decided to find a pay phone and call Kate's home number.

That's when he'd glimpsed her out of the corner of his eye, and the sight had stopped him in his tracks. She was climbing the steps to the diving board of a pool across the lawn from him, perhaps fifty yards away. Lissome and agile, she walked to the end of the board and rose on her tiptoes, extending her arms with the concentration of an Olympian preparing to dive. Only she didn't dive. She did a cannon-ball, just like the kid before her had done.

"What the hell?" Ty breathed.

He watched her swim a few laps, the crawl first, then the backstroke, spurting water like a graceful sea creature, and finally she caught hold of the side of the pool and pulled herself up easily. Water streamed down her back, defining the ripple of feminine muscles in her arms and shoulders. She settled on her haunches for a moment, catching her breath, and when she rose, the slender strength of her legs came into play. *Incredible,* he thought.

Standing in the sunshine, rivulets of water shimmering along the curves of her body, she *was* incredible. He wasn't sure he'd ever seen a woman as toned or supple, except in those health spa ads.

He watched, fascinated, as she walked to a lounge chair beyond the diving board, whisked up a towel and began to dry herself off. She toweled her legs first, and then her stomach and breasts, and finally, she bent over to dry her hair.

She was turned away from him, a three-quarter profile, and the sight of her in that position was almost more than his heart could handle. He sucked in a breath and felt mus-cles tightening in deep dark places. *I'll be dreaming about this for a month,* he thought, a pleasurable heat stroking through his loins. Laughing under his breath, he remem-bered his first accidental glimpse of a naked woman when he was nine. She was a counselor in summer camp, and he'd almost blacked out with the rush of blood from his head. He felt a little like that now—stunned and overstimulated. His heart was pounding. His imagination was igniting with fantasies of Sergeant Kate Madigan's beautiful body spread out beneath him.

He came out of his reverie finally as she gave her head one final shake, straightened and turned, tossing the towel onto the tile beside the lounge chair. The languor with which she draped her arm over her head had an almost wanton quality to it. So did the graceful curve of her belly and the way her breasts swelled from the sides of her bathing suit. The pressure in Ty's groin spiked automatically, and yet it was her facial expression that claimed his attention. She was smiling. It was tentative, a little melancholy, but it was a smile, and that struck him as meaningful. He could count the times he'd seen her smile, they'd been so rare.

Maybe the gods were with him today, he decided, a plan taking form in his mind. She was sunbathing, smiling. More than enough incentive, given that he wasn't a man who needed a great deal of encouragement anyway. Laughing softly, he took cover behind the bush that fronted her apartment and began to unbutton his shirt. One of the timesaving tips he'd learned as a recruit—wearing his workout trunks under his khakis—was going to come in very handy today.

A shuffling sound caught his attention as he was pulling off his pants. He glanced up to see a woman jogging up the path, straight for him. "Twenty-five E," she called out, huffing as she went by him. It took him a minute to figure out that she'd just given him her apartment number.

After stashing his uniform and shoes on Kate's porch, Ty crossed the grass and entered the swimming area through the wrought iron gate. Across the Olympic-size pool from him, her eyes closed, one arm still flung above her head, Kate Madigan seemed to be asleep—or at least pleasantly adrift.

The pool was unoccupied at her end, except for a rotund man bouncing precariously on the diving board, who looked as though he'd empty the pool if he ever jumped. Watching him run up to the end of the board, stop short and teeter like a circus clown, Ty realized he wasn't going to jump. He was performing for the laughing woman sitting alongside the pool.

A shout echoed through Ty's head as he dived into the water. It was the woman hollering at the heavyset man to jump. Swooshing along the bottom, Ty covered half the distance of the pool before he collided with something incredibly large and solid. A whale was his last thought before everything went black.

When Ty came to, someone was kissing him, fervently, and pummeling his chest. Groggily, he lifted an arm and looped it around his passionate attacker. "Have we met?" he asked, slurring his words drunkenly.

"I should have let you drown," a woman whispered angrily in his ear.

There was something menacingly familiar about that voice. Ty's eyes felt as if they were glued shut, but he managed to open them to the blur of feminine features above him.

Gradually the face came into focus, and Ty almost wished it hadn't. Kate Madigan wasn't smiling anymore. "What are you doing in *my* pool?" she said under her breath. Her slate-gray eyes were like two thunderheads. Several other people were huddled around her, staring down at him. A couple of them expressed open concern about her verbal abuse of this poor, half-drowned man.

A paroxysm of coughing came over Ty. As water erupted from his lungs, Kate rolled him onto his side and proceeded to pound on his back.

"Easy," he gasped through a spurt of pool water. He collapsed back, weakened, realizing for the first time that he *had* almost drowned.

"Maybe someone should call an ambulance?" a bystander suggested.

"No," Ty rasped.

"No," Kate seconded simultaneously. "That won't be necessary. I know CPR."

"Boy does she," Ty said, struggling to sit up. "See folks, I'm fine."

"Good," Kate said sharply, "then you'll be able to get in your car and drive away from here, *far* away."

Drive away? Ty sank back to his elbow, coughing and gagging. He had several more relapses before he finally got to his feet, with Kate's help. When she suggested that he rest in a lounge chair, he shuddered violently and complained of the cold. "I could sure use some hot tea and a blanket to wrap up in," he told her.

"Hot tea? Where am I going to get hot tea?" she snapped incredulously. "We are *not* going to my apartment."

Twenty minutes later he was wrapped up in an afghan on her living room couch, and she was serving him steaming hot herbal tea, a malevolent expression on her face.

Ty sipped the brownish brew and nodded wryly. "Hemlock?"

"Lucky for you I'm fresh out. That's Irish moss tea. It's one of my mother's secret weapons."

"Moss? Well that would explain the taste. But it's good and hot," he added diplomatically. "Thanks." He thought he saw a smile flit across her features as she positioned herself at the far end of the couch and remained standing. Realizing she could well have revenge in mind, he pointed to the tea. "What's this stuff going to do to me?"

"Clear your sinuses, unplug your ears." She shrugged. "Actually, I'm not sure what all it does, but my mother swears it's good for just about anything that ails you."

Ty smiled and continued sipping. It was Mother Madigan's *daughter* that ailed him. And he doubted Irish moss tea was the antidote. She'd slipped on a cotton cover-up over her suit, and the T-shirt effect was all very prim and proper except for the way it clung to the damp places on her body and the fact that its over-large neckline was threatening to slide off her shoulder. Ty found that possibility incredibly stimulating.

"If you think you've recovered enough," she said, folding her arms, "I'd like to know what it was you were doing in my pool?"

He rubbed his shoulder, his neck. "A massage would sure be nice about now. I think I've got a little whiplash—"

"Don't tempt me, Raphaell. If I got my hands on your neck—"

He set the teacup down. "Actually, I was swimming across the pool to tell you something."

"Such as?"

"First I want your word that you won't go for your gun. One brush with death in a day is enough for any man."

She shook her head and sighed. "Death is too good for you, Raphaell. What have you *done*?"

For one brief, crazy second, Ty considered coming clean and telling her everything—not just the problems he'd had with Tommy that morning, but the real reason he was taking the reserve training, as well. Luckily, sanity intervened. He couldn't tell her about his research. He'd been ambivalent about his own motives lately, especially where the study was concerned. No, it was too explosive an issue to bring up until he'd decided whether to proceed with it or not.

Compromising, he told her about what had happened that morning, briefly explaining that he'd written her name on his notes, among other things, and that Tommy had caught him.

"Tommy?" Her face lost its color and she sank to the arm of the couch. "What happened? What did he say?"

"He called me into his office after class and read me out royally." Recounting Tommy's tirade, Ty finished by trying to reassure her. "I think I convinced him it was nothing, a one-sided attraction. Student falls in love with teacher, that sort of thing."

"You were writing my name on your *notebook*?" she said, a soft moan in the question. "How could you do that? Only love-struck kids do that!"

He glanced down at the tea, up at her, and finally he spoke. "That's what you do to me, Sarge."

There was a huskiness in his voice, and they both heard it. She flushed with annoyance, and something else he might have read as desire in a woman less angry. Or was it desire? he wondered, staring at her. Even after today?

The emotions tumbling around inside Kate were much more complex than that. She was furious at him for doing this to her. But she was even more furious at him for almost *dying* on her. She'd felt abject terror when she'd seen his body floating at the bottom of her pool. A craziness had overwhelmed her, a desperate need to save him, and with it a crashing realization. She didn't want to lose him. *Please God, don't take him away from me, too,* she'd thought as she'd tried to breathe life back into him, tears burning her eyelids. At that moment she had loved him—a man she barely knew—and she'd relived all the heartrending pain that comes with loss.

But then he'd swung his arm around her neck, kissed her and mumbled some smart-aleck comment in her ear. She'd reeled back in shock, certain she'd been taken in. He'd been acting! That's when the fury had hit her. That's when she'd wanted to throttle him with her bare hands for terrifying her, and for making her cry and pray and feel such desperation.

It wasn't until he'd coughed up the water that she believed he really had lost consciousness in the pool. That's when the confusion hit. That's when she wasn't sure what she felt anymore. And now, standing across the room from him, staring at him wrapped up in the pink afghan her mother had crocheted, his hair all tousled and glossy dark, his eyes a vivid green under damp, spiked lashes—now she'd begun to feel it again. That flicker of dread. That sense of having almost lost him.

It was insane. How could she feel this way about him? It frightened the hell out of her, because she knew that kind of loss was rooted in love, and she didn't want to feel *love* for this man. She *couldn't* let herself feel love for this man. It was crazy and irresponsible. It was professional suicide.

His voice cut through her thoughts. "I guess I said the wrong thing?"

"What do you mean, that's what I do to you?" she came back, a soft accusation in the question. "No, stay there! *Don't get up,*" she cried as he let the afghan slide from around his shoulders. He hesitated on the couch, but the sight of him, bare-chested and frozen in the act of coming toward her was terrifying to Kate.

"What do I mean?" His eyes brushed over her, and their intent was stunningly intimate. "I mean you make me feel like I can't quite catch my breath sometimes. You make me want to write your name in my notebook and carve our initials on trees." Exhaling harsh laughter he stood up. "God, I even dream about you, Kate Madigan."

She raised her hand, deterring him. "Raphaell, *no*—we can't do this. If you don't care whether or not they suspend you, then please think about me. My job is at stake." She heard the plea in her voice. She felt it and meant it, but in the back of her mind, she kept hearing another voice, *his...I even dream about you, Kate Madigan.*

The flash of longing she felt was sudden and sharply physical. It was a tremor sweeping across her skin and a sweet flaring ache deep in her bones. It shook her to the core.

"Raphaell, *please...*" she whispered, closing her eyes for a moment, breathing in deeply, "you have to leave."

His answer was silence, pulsing silence. When he finally spoke, it was with careful control. "You're sure that's what you want."

"Yes, *go, please*." Moments later, as she opened her eyes, he was buttoning the shirt of his uniform. She turned away, stiffening as he came up behind her.

"I told myself I was coming here to tell you about Tommy," he admitted quietly. "But that's not really why I'm here. I just wanted to see you again."

She whirled and looked up at him, a kind of sadness closing off her throat. "Don't say things like that. Don't tell me you just wanted to see me again. You have no right." She felt the heat behind her eyelids, the stinging threat of tears. Oh God, she didn't want to cry, didn't want him to see her cry.

He touched her face, and she could see her own sadness shadowed in his eyes. "Thanks for saving my life, Sarge. Is it okay to say that?"

The flicker of emotion in his voice brought a quick, piercing pain to her throat. *Don't care about me, Raphaell, please. Don't love me. It will kill me if you do.*

The tears welled and she blinked them away. His shadowed eyes were so beautiful to her in her anguished state of awareness, more beautiful than anything she'd ever seen. The longing that stirred inside her grew more poignant and urgent with every gentle stroke of his fingers on her cheek. She wanted him to hold her again, to dream with her while they danced to love songs. She wanted him to sweep her up and carry her off, away from all the rules and regulations, all the policies and procedures.

"Is it against the law for me to kiss you goodbye," he asked, "one last time?"

She turned away, a sigh of anguish in her throat. "Yes."

His voice seemed faraway when he spoke. "I promised last night I wouldn't hurt you—"

Whatever else he was going to say was cut off by a loud thumping on the front door. Both he and Kate swung around and froze as a man's voice called out, "Kate? It's Tommy!"

Chapter Eight

Tommy?" Kate gasped softly, turning to Ty. "If he finds you here—"

"He won't. Is there another way out of this apartment?"

"The bedroom has a patio door."

"Okay. Give me a couple of minutes before you let him in." He took her hand and hesitated. "Maybe I ought to stay? If he gives you a hard time—"

"Raphaell, *go*," she said abruptly. "I'm coming, Tommy!" she called out as the pounding increased.

Kate pressed the back of her fingers to her lips as she watched Raphaell disappear into the bedroom. She heard him open and shut the patio door behind him, and then she counted out fifteen seconds, walked to the front door and opened it.

"Hi, Haggerty," she said, her voice wavering as she summoned a smile.

Tommy stared at her a moment, without even a hint of an answering smile. "Can I come in?"

"Sure," she said, too brightly.

He walked past her and halted next to the sofa, studying the teacup on the coffee table. "They said you were sick."

"Yes, a headache." She hated the stiffness, the awkwardness between them. "I was just having some tea. Can I get you some?"

He shook his head and was silent. Kate sensed the purposeful momentum in him. He'd come for a reason, but there was a tentativeness there as well, as though he didn't quite know what he was supposed to do next.

"Tommy," she said quietly, "why are you here?"

"I don't know. I thought you might be . . . in trouble."

"Trouble?"

He stared at her cover-up, his eyes on the bikini visible through the thin white cotton. "What the hell's going on, Kate?"

Kate felt the tug of confusing emotions . . . regret, remorse, denial. She looked away from him at the very moment when she knew he expected her to meet his eyes, to tell him the truth. "Nothing's going on. I woke up with a headache."

"Headache," he muttered, tacking on an expletive that pointedly conveyed his frustration. "Raphaell didn't show up at the firing range this afternoon. I suppose you don't know anything about that?"

"Why would I? I've been here all day."

He was so quiet that Kate forced herself to look at him finally—and saw the distress in his leathery features. "Dammit, Tommy," she said, her voice cracking, "nothing's going on. What are you trying to say?"

His eyes were sad and angry. They told her he knew, and suddenly she couldn't pretend any longer. "All right, Raphaell *was* here, but it isn't what you think. He had an accident. He nearly drowned in the pool. I had to—''

"What was he doing here?"

"He just wanted me to know that you'd called him to your office. He said he told you there was nothing between us." She shrugged awkwardly. "Him and me, I mean."

"*Is* there something between you?"

Kate felt the confusion, the conflict welling up inside her again, fraying her overwrought nerves. She stared at him, swallowing hard, shaking her head. "I don't know."

"*Kate,*" he breathed, an urgency in his gruff voice, "there's only one right answer to that question, and it's *no.*" He reached her instantly, took hold of her hand and shook it gently like he might have a disobedient child's. "There isn't anything between you and Raphaell, Kate. There can't be, and you know it. There's too much at stake, the promotion, your *job.* Everything you've worked for—"

"I danced with him last night, Tommy," she blurted, aware of his grip tightening on her hand. Suddenly, inexplicably, tears stung her eyes. "I danced with him, and then he kissed me."

Disbelief crashed over Tommy's face like a wave. "Good God, Kate," he whispered, "have you gone crazy?"

She twisted away from him and walked to the window, staring out, down at the pool, remembering Raphaell's body floating on the bottom, remembering her desperation. A wave of anguish swept over her. Yes, she had gone crazy. She *was* crazy. "It's worse than that, Tommy," she said, her voice barely audible. "I have these feelings, and they're so strong."

"Feelings? What does that mean? What are you *saying*, Kate?"

"I don't know...."

She heard him moving, shifting.

"No way," he mumbled to himself. "She can't be saying what I think she's saying. Kate...tell me I'm wrong. You're not in love with this guy, are you? God, not one of your own recruits?"

The grainy, beseeching quality of his question tore at her control. "I'm sorry," she whispered, turning to him, her chin trembling. "Oh, Tommy, I'm sorry." The regret that welled inside her was as much for him as for herself. He had trained her, and in his gruff, reticent way, he had taken pride in everything she'd done. He'd never told her, that wasn't his way, but she'd seen it in his eyes. Now, all she could see was his disappointment, his sadness and it brought her such pain.

"I know this is a terrible mess," she said, looking away, blinking against the sting of tears. "I don't want to have these feelings. I don't know why I do. I don't know how any of this *happened*."

Suddenly he was there, next to her.

"Hey, hey," he said brusquely, as though embarrassed at his own emotion, "don't be crying now. Come on, Storm," he coaxed, pulling her into his arms stiffly, patting her back with quick, gentle thumps. "Don't cry on me, please. I don't know what the hell to do when a woman cries."

"I won't," she promised, rasping out the words. "I'm all right, Tommy, really, I am."

"Ah, the hell you say," he muttered, pulling her closer. A sharp aching flared in Kate's throat as she fought against the emotion cresting inside her. "Tommy, don't," she pleaded, stiffening in his arms. But he wouldn't release her, and finally his roughened tenderness toppled what was left of her self-control. Her breath caught on a dragged-in sob.

"No, I'm not," she whispered, pressing her forehead against his chest, tears locked in her throat, tears streaming hotly down her cheeks. "No, I'm not all right. Oh God, Tommy, what am I going to do?"

Sighing, patting the back of her head with his hand, he said, "I think you're gonna cry for a while."

He held her like a father would a child, soothing her until she was quiet, and even then, he continued to rock her almost as though it gave him some kind of comfort, too. At last he cleared his throat and held her at arm's length. "You got that out of your system?"

She nodded.

"Okay, then," he said, grimacing as he knuckled away the dampness from her cheeks, "I guess it's my turn." His eyes narrowed in the no-nonsense stare that had made him famous.

"Listen up, Madigan, because I'm only going to say this once. You think you're confused, but you're not, you hear me? You know exactly what you're going to do. You're going to snap back like a double-thick rubber band. You're going to tell that Romeo of a recruit to stay the hell away from you, or *I'll* tell him. We can't bounce him from the academy without dragging you into it, but I'll deal with him—"

"Tommy," she stopped him, "this isn't Raphaell's fault."

"It's not anybody's fault," he said, conveying a depth of understanding she hadn't expected, and perhaps didn't deserve. "Hell, I'm as much to blame as he is, or you," he muttered. "I saw it coming, and I didn't do anything. I talked you into the damn dart game, and then I left the two of you there in the bar—not once, but twice." He released her, hesitating, and then he exhaled heavily. "We've never talked about it, Kate. But I know what it's been like for you since Glenn died. I know how lonely a cop's life is."

"Don't—" She shook her head, a sudden sharpness in her breathing. In his awkward way, he was touching upon things that hurt too much, and if he kept it up, she would soon be in tears again.

"You can't let this rock you, Kate. I never thought I'd hear myself making speeches like this, but the simple truth is you've worked too long and too hard. You've got too much to lose. Hey, come on," he said, taking her hand, shaking it gently, "have you forgotten? Tomorrow's the big day."

She looked up at him. "Big day?"

"The inspection, Kate."

"Oh God," she whispered, closing her eyes, nodding. It wasn't that she'd forgotten the inspection. It was just that with the emotional turmoil of the last twenty-four hours, the inspection, the academy, all of the things that had preoccupied her for so many years, had slipped into the back of her awareness. They barely felt real to her.

When she opened her eyes, Tommy was staring at her, hard. "I'm no flag-waver, Kate, you know that, but the platoon needs you now. Those kids look up to you, especially MacGregor. You can't let them down. You can't let *her* down."

Kate's features tightened, and a kind of pain stung her jaw. Of course he was right.

The tension on the Grinder the next morning was thick enough to grease a truck axle as the recruits checked out each others' uniforms and gear and began to form ranks for the big moment. The youngest male recruit in the group had been unlucky enough to rotate into the class sergeant position for that particular day, and he and his squad leaders were anxiously taking their positions in front of the assembly. It was their job to have the platoon in formation and ready for the inspection by the time the D.I.s arrived.

"Your knot's loose," Ty said, standing next to MacGregor in the last rank. He tweaked her tie and winked at her. "Sergeant Madigan's going to rain on your parade for that."

"Right," MacGregor agreed wryly, "it must be too loose. I'm not strangling yet." She tightened the knot, her eyes bulging comically. Ty laughed, and she took a swipe at his fanny. "Lint," she said, grinning at him.

"Watch that, MacGregor," he warned, glancing at her backside. "I'm a pretty good lint-remover myself."

"Promises, promises." Her smile was sweetly provocative.

"Wonder where the Screamin' Blue Meanie is?" a recruit questioned, his voice carrying over the general confusion.

"Probably polishing her gun," another retorted.

Ty glanced toward the academy's administration building. He wondered where she was, too. And why she hadn't answered his telephone calls. He'd had a restless night wondering what had happened between her and Tommy. He'd even shown up early this morning and stopped by her office, only to be shooed away by the secretary and told Sergeant Madigan hadn't arrived yet.

"I heard Madigan's up for a promotion," MacGregor said, breaking into Ty's thoughts.

"Promotion?"

MacGregor nodded. "Executive training adviser, Buchanan's job. She'd be the first, you know. The academy's never had a woman E.T.A. before." MacGregor nodded wisely, a font of information. "I guess this inspection's probably real important to her, white gloves and everything. The big brass are going to be here."

Ty grew silent again. Why hadn't Kate told him? God, he'd had no idea what was at stake for her today.

"Here they come," somebody whispered.

"Ten*shun*!" the class sergeant barked. Ty sucked in a breath and his head snapped up. His eyes front, he caught a glimpse of Kate and Tommy walking toward them in his peripheral vision.

When she came into his direct line of sight, his chest tightened. She was lovely, her pale skin drawn tight over her cheekbones. He'd never seen her so beautiful—or so tentative. She seemed hesitant, unsure of herself, even a little bewildered. Tommy, next to her, looked ready to chew up the platoon and spit it out. The D.I. was visually searching the ranks, and his eyes glittered with warning menace as he focused on Ty. *He knows,* Ty thought, locking in tight on the piece of sky in front of him. But how much? Ty wondered. And what was coming next?

The next several minutes crawled by as the last of the parents and spectators arrived, filling up the small stand of bleachers behind Kate and Tommy. A hush fell over the crowd as the dean of the academy and the other brass arrived.

"Dress right, *dress*," the class sergeant snapped, giving the recruits the order to align themselves. The platoon responded instantly and with military precision, extending their left arms, just touching the shoulder of the recruit next to them. "Ready, *front*," the sergeant called out next, finishing the command.

The squad leaders took over and put their individual squads through their paces. Ty felt a flash of pride as the recruits pulled off drill after drill without a hitch. They were putting on a good show for the brass, and the credit would, and *should*, be Kate's. Everybody knew how hard she'd worked for this platoon, how she'd pressured and prodded and *shamed* them into shape.

He was silently rooting for her as she stepped forward and called out the command for the inspection of firearms. "Inspection, *arms*!"

In sync with the other recruits, Ty unsnapped his shoulder strap, grasped the butt of his gun and drew it out, preparing it for inspection. *Give 'em hell, Storm,* he thought, doing his damnedest to keep his eyes front as she stepped to the first recruit, took his gun and began her white glove inspection.

He could hear the waver in her voice as she questioned the recruit. His eyes front, Ty fought the urge to glance her way, to reassure himself that she was okay. Finally, as she moved on to the next recruit, he told himself that it was just a temporary case of the jitters. She was nervous. Who wouldn't be nervous with the dean of the academy staring down your neck? he reasoned. But he could feel his own neck muscles tightening, the tension in his gut.

She'll hit her stride, he told himself, wanting to believe it. Through it all, he was peripherally aware that Tommy was still shooting visual bullets at him.

Ty started as a clatter of noise hit his ears. Several of the recruits' heads snapped in the direction of the commotion, and a buzz rose from the startled crowd. Ty held position, straining with his peripheral vision to see what had happened. A gun lay on the ground, and Kate was bending to pick it up, her hands unsteady. *God*, she'd dropped it, he realized.

Rigidly holding position, Ty watched her, saw her rise with the gun, clutching it in her gloved fingers. Her face was stained with self-reproach.

"Eyes *front!*" Tommy bellowed, bringing the platoon back to attention.

Ty's heart thudded in his chest. She was already shaky. Would she be able to recover from this? He felt the pull of warring needs inside him. He wanted to help her, reassure her, but he knew any gesture on his part, even the blink of an eye at this point, would only compromise her more. She had to be perceived as being totally in charge. As she painstakingly repeated the procedure, Ty's jaw locked with his own frustration. What he would give to play God right now, to find some way to erase what had happened and let her start clean. *Just let her get through this,* he prayed silently.

She *did* get through the inspection without any more terrible blunders, but she was never fully in command. She was not the Sergeant Madigan that had whipped an entire platoon into shape by the sheer force of her will. Ty knew it. They all knew it. Her fire and pride seemed blunted, and it was painful for Ty to witness.

Several things became clear to him in the course of that morning, the most significant of which was that Kate Madigan was altogether human and vulnerable. He realized as never before that her tough facade was a professional survival mechanism, a way to endure the rigors of the job. She needed that toughness to survive, and he'd been systematically undermining it ever since he met her. Yes, she was vulnerable, and by his relentless determination to get to that aspect of her, he'd shaken her defenses.

He didn't have to be told what had happened between her and Tommy last night. He knew. There'd been a confrontation, a confession. He also knew that today's disaster didn't need to have happened. If he'd backed off when she'd asked him to, if he hadn't gone to her apartment, it *wouldn't* have happened. *I did this to her,* he thought.

A dull ache flared along his jaw as muscles contracted. He'd pulled a few stunts in his life, done some things he wasn't proud of, and he regretted those occasions. But nothing like he regretted this. He'd hurt her, maybe even jeopardized her chances for the promotion.

As she proceeded through the ranks and finally reached him, he wanted to tell her he understood now that it was her life and her profession he'd been playing with. He wanted to tell her he was *sorry*.

She took the .357 magnum from his hands, a brittleness in her movements. The pale beauty, the gripping intensity in her features brought a sharp pain to his breathing. She was

fighting for control. She was fighting to get through this
ordeal, and there was nothing he could do.

A thought blared in his head. *You can leave her alone,
Raphaell, that's what you can do.* The warning was loud,
sharp, as though someone had spiked the volume on a
powerful sound system. Ty knew it for the truth. There was
only one way he could help her now, and that was by back-
ing off, by staying out of her personal life. The decision
turned his gut into a fist.

By the time she'd finished with his gun and handed it back
to him, he had resolved the problem in his mind, if not in his
heart. He would stay the hell away from her. He would stop
interfering with her professionally and emotionally.

Ruthlessly ignoring the hollow sensation in his chest, he
convinced himself that there were other reasons to back off.
He had to make a decision about his study, for one thing.
He'd been neglecting the research, and if he intended to go
on with it, he couldn't waste any more time.

From now on it would be by the book, he thought. He
would address her as ma'am, salute her, speak to her only
with permission.

Except to apologize, he thought. He owed her that.

Kate sprinted through the darkness, her running shoes
pounding on the soft turf, the impact of each stride rever-
berating through her body. She was breathing hard, running hard, physically and emotionally battering away at her
own pervasive sense of failure.

She'd relived the inspection in her mind a hundred times:
the dropped gun, the unforgivable shakiness, the dean's
courteous but cool response to her afterward. She'd blown
it, that was all. Whether she'd blown the promotion along
with it, she didn't know. But her chances had to have been
hurt significantly. She'd seen it in the dean's eyes, and she'd

heard it in the false cheer in Tommy's voice when he'd tried to reassure her afterward.

The rest of the day had been a nightmare she barely remembered. She'd gone through the motions, and as soon as she'd finished her last class and the day's paperwork, she'd suited up and begun to run, far more concerned with her need to purge herself of the suffocating sense of failure than with the minimal risks of running at nightfall on the campus.

She was on her fourth mile now, and her body's demands for oxygen and energy were beginning to override the gnawing tension in her stomach. Concentrating on her breathing, on the hypnotic rhythm of her strides, she rounded the academy's parking lot and entered the workout yard, taking a short cut through the cropped grass. Go for five, she thought, remembering the line she'd used as a recruit to keep herself going. *One more mile for the academy.* A grimace, bittersweet, flicked across her lips.

She reached the asphalt path that led into the campus and noticed a figure standing by the obstacle course's seven-foot wall several yards in front of her. Pulling up, breathing hard, she dug into the pocket of her shorts for her key chain. With the miniature baton clutched in her hand, she slowed up and began to walk, her eyes on him as he moved toward her and into the light.

Recognition jolted her nerves, her heart. *"Raphaell?"* She halted, her voice tight with emotion. "What are you doing here?" God, it hurt her just to *look* at him.

"Why didn't you tell me you were up for a promotion?" he asked, nearing her.

"Would it have made a difference?" She couldn't stop the question—or blunt its edgy pain.

He hesitated a few feet away, as though he sensed that to come nearer would antagonize her. In the thin moonlight, his features looked like a pensive charcoal sketch, dramatically shadowed and grave. She couldn't see his eyes and she was profoundly grateful for that.

"What do you want?" she asked.

"To apologize. It must have been hell out there this morning. If any part of that was my fault—" Taking a deep breath, he raked a hand through his hair. "No, it *was* my fault, all of it, and I'm sorry."

"Sorry?" She hadn't expected that, an apology. *She didn't want an apology.* All she wanted was to stop the sharpness that was cutting into her heart.

"Are you going to be okay?"

The question was so loaded with concern, with solicitous doubt, that it made her indignant. And the welling anger, *blessed* anger, gave her strength. "Of course I am," she said, clipping the words off, ruthlessly forcing the emotion from her voice. "I'm the D.I., Raphaell. I'm the one responsible, for all of it, including the fiasco today."

"The buck stops here, huh?"

"That's right." She shoved her keys back into her pocket and swiped at a trickle of perspiration that was rolling down her cheek. "Now, if you'll get out of my way, I'd like to finish my run."

She started past him, gasping softly as he caught her by the arm.

"It's okay," he said, staying her for a moment, his voice low, heavy with conviction. "I just want you to know you don't have to worry about me anymore. It'll be strictly by the book from now on." He tightened his grip for one brief, possessive second. "You have my word on that."

She stared up at him and some wordless emotion pierced her. She couldn't express it. She didn't understand it. Suddenly tears were burning her eyelids…and the emotion had a name. The same anguish she'd felt that first night at the bar suffused her throat. Then it had been beautiful and painful. Now she felt only the pain. Dear God, what was happening to her? she wondered. What gave this man the ability to elicit such emotion from her? *What was his power?*

Wrenching away from him, she ran.

Chapter Nine

Kate was a reluctant visitor to the valley of broken dreams and broken hearts. Profoundly uncomfortable with emotional upheaval in any form, she forced herself to rally quickly. The next morning she was back in class, teaching. That night, she joined Tommy and some of the other D.I.s for pizza, and by the following morning she was back on the Grinder snapping out orders again.

She needn't have worried about losing her edge. If anything, her commands were a little too sharp. She was tired, she told herself, and understandably shaken by the events of the last few days, but she knew that was only part of the reason she felt so raw and edgy inside. She presented a bold, bluff front to everyone at the academy, including Tommy, but underneath it she was a tangle of exposed nerves.

Her one-day recovery would have been considered a quick comeback by any normal standard of behavior. By Kate's standards it was a lifetime, a twenty-four hour walk in the wilderness. Finally, beset by angst, self-doubt and confusion, she grabbed tight for her old values and convictions and held on fast. There is a lesson in all of this, she told herself repeatedly. When you feel like breaking rules, running in the rain and being bad, *don't*.

At last it was her grandpop who came to the rescue. He had another way of handling life's setbacks, Kate remembered. *The only failure is giving up*, he used to say.

Kate was to remind herself of that wisdom many times in the days that followed. The rumors around campus were that she had lost the promotion. It was only gossip, she knew, and yet the whispers hit her like body blows. She dealt with the disappointment by digging in, by focusing on the upcoming finals. She owed her platoon that at least. *She* had fluffed the formal inspection, not they. "You guys are going to be the best graduating class this academy's ever seen," she promised them so often that the words took on the fervor of a fight song.

The remaining few weeks of class passed quickly. The recruits worked hard under Kate's tutelage, and Ty's behavior in particular was exemplary. She wasn't sure exactly when it was that she had realized he would be the O.R., but when she'd admitted it to herself finally it had rocked her with a kind of sadness. Even now the thought brought her a moment of heartache. How would she feel presenting him with the award that she, herself, had won ten years before?

Something else was bothering her about Raphaell—had been for weeks—but she was loathe to admit it, even to herself. Occasionally, in a weak moment, she had found herself wondering how he'd managed to be so cooperative, so damn military. He hadn't once given her a suggestive glance, made an untoward move, or even looked like he wanted to. She should have been grateful. She wasn't. Oh, maybe at first, when she'd been fighting her own demons, but eventually doubts had crept in. He'd promised her it would be by the book, but she hadn't expected him to keep that promise so easily. It was as though they'd never been close, never shared stolen moments of laughter and passion. It was, she realized, *as though he had never cared*.

That thought was too hurtful for Kate to contemplate.

Grateful that she had other pressing concerns, she immersed herself in the cause of getting the recruits, and particularly Melissa MacGregor, ready for the battery of exams they would have to take. MacGregor was still struggling with some of the physical strength requirements, and Kate wasn't at all optimistic that she could master them quickly enough to pass the fitness exam. She still hadn't successfully completed the body drag, and she hadn't managed to shoulder throw even the lightest of the male recruits in the weaponless defense class.

Two days before the finals, Kate found MacGregor in the gymnasium, practicing her side and back kicks for the self-defense class scheduled that morning.

"You ready to slay some dragons today?" Kate asked.

"Yes, ma'am," MacGregor said, laughing. "Point me to 'em. I'll have 'em feet up and squealing for mercy."

Kate returned the recruit's smile. "Confidence, MacGregor. I like that."

Moments later, lecturing the class, Kate told the recruits bluntly that the moves they were about to learn could mean the difference between life and death. "So stay tuned, ladies and gentlemen," she advised.

First she reviewed the vulnerable areas of the body and the various methods of attack, emphasizing that in self-defense, it was speed and accuracy that counted, not brute strength. Then she asked for a volunteer and demonstrated release moves and counterattack strategy. Finally, she ordered the class to pair up and position themselves on the large mats that covered the gym floor.

"Let's see the rear-attack choke release first," she said, walking through the class. "Remember, once you've made the decision to counterattack, get behind it *one hundred percent*. Use full force.''

Walking and observing, Kate called out tips as the recruits tried various release strategies. MacGregor and Raphaell had paired up on a mat near the back wall, and as Kate neared them, she watched Raphaell come at MacGregor from behind and apply the choke hold. Grunting, MacGregor quickly turned into his elbow, twisted toward his body and disabled him with a simulated groin punch. Raphaell doubled over, feigning a grimace of pain as he muttered something about his future children.

"Good job, MacGregor," Kate said, her glance colliding with Raphaell's for just a fraction of a second. His slow smile startled her. It made her heart feel funny. *It made her want to smile back*. "That was, uh...pretty good," she said quickly. "Okay, let's see the shoulder throw next."

Again, Raphaell came at MacGregor from behind and applied the choke hold. MacGregor immediately grasped his arms, dropped to her knees and tugged frantically, but she wasn't able to flip him over her shoulder.

Kate felt a twist of frustration. The strategy behind the shoulder throw was to catch the attacker off balance, to go against his expectation of resistance by dropping to the knees. Once even a large man's equilibrium was disrupted, it was a fairly simple thing to somersault him over the shoulder. MacGregor's problem, Kate realized, was not physical, but psychological. The recruit didn't believe she could do it.

"MacGregor," Kate said evenly, "you're trying too hard. The trick is to fall forward, to let the body flow the way it's made to flow." Motioning MacGregor aside, she stepped onto the mat. "Raphaell, come at me from behind."

"With pleasure," he said under his breath.

Kate picked up the murmured comment, but she didn't have time to respond to it. He moved quickly to lock his arm around her neck, and she reacted instantaneously. Gripping his arm and plummeting forward, she gracefully flipped his body over hers in one fluid movement.

As Raphaell hit the mat, applause broke out from the recruits that had stopped to watch.

"Outstanding," MacGregor murmured, staring down at Raphaell's supine body. "And he's so *big*, too."

"The bigger they are," Raphaell muttered, propping himself on his elbows, irony in his voice.

Kate suppressed a smile. He looked irresistible lying there on the mat in his workout sweats, an upended Goliath. Again their eyes connected for an instant, and this time her heart jumped painfully. Something is happening here, she thought. He's giving off different signals. *Is he flirting with me?* "Okay, MacGregor," she said, a slight catch in her voice, "now show me you can do it."

"The question is," Raphaell countered, pushing to his feet, "can *I* do it?"

The entire class crowded around to watch as Raphaell approached the young female recruit from the back and swung an arm around her neck. Kate saw MacGregor tense, her body locking up almost immediately.

"Go with it, MacGregor! Fall forward!" Kate coached as the young woman grasped for her attacker's arm. "Put him off balance, make his body weight work against him! *You can do it!*"

With an anguished groan, MacGregor dropped to her knees and lurched forward, but she simply didn't have the momentum to complete the throw. Wailing with sudden fury, she reared up, dropped again and this time she hoisted Raphaell's weight right over her body. Not easily, not gracefully, but she did it, and the entire class roared their approval.

Kate let out a tight sigh of relief and a grin broke on her face. "Atta girl," she said, shooting MacGregor a thumbs-up. She turned away from the picture of the young woman and the star recruit, both sitting on the mat staring up at her, the first with a pleased smile, the second with a much more threatening message hidden in his expression—male interest. Raphaell didn't need weaponless defense, Kate thought. He had those *eyes*.

"Okay, you beanbags," she yelled at the gawkers, "let's see *you* do it!"

Before the class was over, MacGregor had caught on to the essential factor, belief in herself, and she was flinging recruits around with abandon. Raphaell was throwing all takers, too. But then, Kate had never been worried about him. At least not when it came to weaponless defense.

The morning of the physical fitness test arrived with overcast skies and anxious spirits. Standing on the workout yard, Kate was almost as nervous as the recruits were. She watched with a clenched jaw as MacGregor strained to pull the 165-pound dummy thirty-two feet within the allotted time. The test required two successful drags. To everyone's astonishment, MacGregor made both of them. After the last, she flashed Kate a triumphant grin, dropped the dummy and leaped straight up into the air.

Next came the 99-yard obstacle course, the event everyone expected Raphaell to take easily. Tommy stood at the starting block with a stopwatch, Kate at the finish line. Raphaell, wearing the school's official blue shorts and T-shirt, shook out his arms and legs, took a couple of deep breaths and positioned himself.

Somewhere along the line, Kate remembered, the platoon had begun calling him the "running machine." Now, watching him, acutely aware of his long, sinewy legs poised for instant action, his narrow hips pivoted forward and his shoulders curved inward, Kate knew why.

Tommy raised his hand, brought it down and popped the stopwatch. Raphaell dug out, burning up the short straightaway, acing the ninety-degree turn, vaulting the first obstacle easily. He made the next turn and the next, vaulting, running, vaulting again until finally he hit the double jump, a six-inch curb followed by a four-foot fence.

Kate watched him clear the curb, then gather together like a coiled spring and leap the fence. It was a dazzling sight, primal in some way she understood but couldn't have explained. He was beautiful, animallike in his instinctive agility and mastery of the course. He made the last S-turn easily and flew toward the finish, toward *her*.

Their eyes met as he came straight at her, and Kate's breath caught in her throat.

He wavered for an instant, just a split second in time, but it was enough for his forward thrust to diminish, for the delicate cross signals between brain and body to misfire. His foot came down wrong. It folded underneath him, propelling him forward, and he did a magnificent slide into home *and* into his wide-eyed drill instructor.

"Look out!" someone screamed.

Kate tried to jump back, but the warning came too late. Ty took her down just as a hurricane levels an unsuspecting palm tree. Flat on her back, the wind knocked out of her, Kate saw nothing but stars for several seconds.

Eventually a pair of concerned green eyes came into focus.

"Are you okay?" Ty asked, brushing strands of auburn hair from her face. "Does it hurt anywhere?"

"Uh-huh," she said, staring up at him, managing a smile that must have looked a little loopy. "Everywhere."

He smiled back, his eyes twinkling. "Sorry about that."

"S'okay," she murmured, "I'm tough."

He nodded, inhaled. "Yeah . . . I know. By the way," he added after a moment, "if you'd stayed out a little longer, I was going to resuscitate you."

Resuscitate? Kate's pulse was suddenly erratic, and she doubted the fall had anything to do with it. This man *was* flirting with her. Yes, indeed, and she rather liked it . . . even if it did involve being sacked like a quarterback.

Kate didn't have time to speculate on Ty's behavior any further. Tommy and a flock of recruits rushed to the rescue, whereupon she was checked for broken bones and helped to her feet. She made a remarkably quick recovery, and even with his unorthodox finish, Ty won the obstacle course by a full second.

During the remainder of exam week, Kate was to speculate on Ty Raphaell at much greater length. On those occasions where she did see him—at the firearm qualifications and the written final—he seemed almost subdued. His sudden mood swing confounded her. It was as though he'd broken his own honor code with the flirtations, and now he was doing penance. Or was it something else? she wondered. She'd always sensed some other purpose in him, something held back. Curious, and a little heavy of heart, Kate realized she had so many questions about him and no answers.

As the week ended and Ty remained politely distant, Kate began to wonder if he was feeling the same thing she was, a sense of something inevitable and final, of the road coming to an end. It was almost over, she realized, saddened.

Graduation day dawned a week later, a beautiful bright Saturday morning. Studded with flags and important dignitaries, D.I.s and recruits in full uniform, the academy auditorium was an impressive sight.

As the opening remarks were completed, Kate was summoned to the dais to announce the recruits in her class who were to be honored. She called them up individually, a catch of pride in her voice as she congratulated each one.

Finally it was Raphaell's turn to receive his plaque. He came forward, and Kate reached out to shake his hand, a soft surge of emotion in her throat. "This is the highest honor we have to give, Mr. Raphaell," she said, presenting him with the plaque. "The academy is proud of you . . . and so am I."

His eyes, his smile were sober as she finished her remarks and he took the plaque. "I'm in good company," he said, acknowledging her similar achievement. His gaze brushed over her as he added softly, "It's been a privilege, Sarge."

She nodded, tried to smile back, her lips compressing with emotion as he turned and walked away from her.

Afterward, out on the yard, she watched the jubilant graduates congratulating each other, and the sense of loss she'd been feeling all week deepened. A tight ache encircled her heart as she watched Raphaell pick MacGregor right up off the ground, hug her and swing her around. They looked so joyful it was hard for Kate to watch. They were both moving on to something else, she realized, with a crushing sense of being left behind. It *was* over.

"You want to go get a beer or something?" Tommy asked.

"A beer, Tommy?" She glanced at her watch. "It's not even noon."

"I was going to suggest coffee, but the way you look, I figured something stronger might be in order."

"How do I look?"

"Like a lost puppy."

"Don't be silly," she said, shaken by the concern in his voice. "I'm fine. I'm always a little sad when it's all over. You know how that is. Besides, this was a difficult class."

"It was," he agreed brusquely, as though he intended to say nothing more about that. "What you need, Sergeant Madigan, is some R and R—a good, long rest."

"Rest?" Kate said, smiling faintly. "What does that mean?"

Kate wasn't being entirely facetious. She'd always buried her uncertainties in an avalanche of activity. Work was her answer. Unfortunately, she was soon to learn that work *wasn't* the answer this time, and it took her exactly two days of spinning her wheels to figure that out. One sunny afternoon, sitting at her desk, staring at the files she'd just reorganized, at her shiny, immaculate office, she knew she was only going through the motions.

With the academy in hiatus between classes, and with five years of uninterrupted service behind her, she decided Tommy was right. She desperately needed a change, and some R and R was long overdue. "I'll be fine," she assured Art Buchanan when he looked astonished at her request for a vacation. "I just need a little reassessment time."

Kate spent her first day of leisure poolside, and though soaking up the sun and thumbing through glossy magazines felt wickedly hedonistic, it gave her far too much time to dwell on her thoughts. She thought about MacGregor, about Raphaell. She wondered how MacGregor was doing in her field training with an inland police agency, but it was Raphaell who consumed her preoccupations. She tried to imagine his life outside of their experience at the academy and found that she couldn't. He taught, he wrote, she knew that. But who was he and why had he taken the course?

Sadness lingered, the sense of loss drifting over her like a low-lying cloud as her mind recreated soft, sepia images of their time together. Mostly, she wondered about his change in mood that last week before graduation. What had it meant? She hadn't imagined his reawakened interest, she was sure of that. It was possible he'd expected her to do something, say something. Had he been waiting for her to make the first move? She just didn't know. And now it was too late.

Finally Kate knew she had to put him out of her thoughts. She was sinking deeper and deeper into melancholy dreams of what might have been. Crying over spilled milk had never been her style, and she wasn't about to let it become a habit now. Determined to enjoy her vacation, she indulged herself in all the things she hadn't had time for over the years: lunch at the marina, shopping trips, and finally she even redecorated her bedroom with a new bedspread and clusters of white eyelet pillows. By the time she was done, she had a room that was thoroughly feminine—and all she could think about was how Ty Raphaell would look with his exotic dark hair and features showcased by those ruffled pillows!

Exactly eight days into her unprecedented vacation, on the Saturday before she had to report back to the academy, Kate's preoccupation with Ty Raphaell was abruptly ended by a telephone call from Art Buchanan's secretary.

"Sergeant Madigan?" the woman said. "Mr. Buchanan thought I ought to call you. Melissa MacGregor's been hurt."

"MacGregor? What happened?" Kate asked.

"She's at St. Joseph's hospital. I'm afraid she was wounded in a liquor store shoot-out."

Chapter Ten

Ty Raphaell raked a hand through his hair as he paced the third-floor visitors' lounge at St. Joseph's. He was waiting for the nurse who'd curtly blocked his entry into Melissa MacGregor's room, hauled him off to the waiting room and promised to return with word about the young woman. All they'd told Ty at the desk was that Melissa's condition was listed as fair. He wasn't even sure who'd telephoned the message to his college office that Melissa had been shot.

Suddenly the nurse swung into the lounge's doorway. "You can see Ms. MacGregor now."

"Is she all right?" Ty asked, following the nurse's lead down the hall.

"She's coming along nicely," the nurse assured him. "Apparently, she had quite a lot of excitement this morning. I'll let her tell you about it."

Ty was startled when he entered the room and saw Melissa propped up in bed, a smile on her face. She seemed perfectly healthy. "You're looking good for a cop brought down in her prime by a bullet," he said, standing in the doorway, smiling back at her. "Where'd they get you?"

"Hi, come on in." She waved him toward the bed. "Check this out," she said, pointing toward her foot, which was elevated and thickly dressed in white gauze bandages.

"Somebody shot you in the *foot*, MacGregor? How did that happen?"

Pride warmed MacGregor's smile. "I stopped a robbery in progress."

"You *what*?" He remembered Melissa telling him she was doing her field training with the Glendale police force, but surely they hadn't sent her out on a call like that?

"It was really great," she said, obviously bubbling to tell him. "I was off duty this morning—in my civvies—and I stopped by the Mini-Mart Liquor Store to get a cup of coffee on my way to the health club—" Her quick pause seemed intended to make sure he was getting it all. "Okay, well the suspect was fleeing the scene, and he took me hostage."

"Damn," Ty murmured softly. "How'd you get out of that?"

She grinned. "The shoulder throw? It works."

"You flipped an armed robber?"

"Just like Sergeant Madigan taught us. The guy had me in a choke hold and was dragging me toward the door when the liquor store owner went for his gun. That took the suspect's mind off me for a second—" she shrugged "—so I dropped to my knees and 'Ally Ooped' him. Trouble is, his gun went off as he was going over. He got me in the foot."

"Oh my God," Ty said, shaking his head and trying not to laugh, "only you, MacGregor, *only* you."

As she went on to describe the scene in detail, Ty thought about the information he'd been feeding into his computer over the last months, the data he'd accumulated for his study. His own experience with an abusive D.I. in the army had been the driving force behind his desire to expose the negative effects of "stress" training. But now, staring at MacGregor, he realized she'd not only brought down a robbery suspect, she'd probably saved herself and the store owner from serious injury, possibly even death, *because* of her training.

"You did well, MacGregor," Ty observed. "You used your head."

"I did, didn't I?" She grinned modestly. "I stayed cool in the face of adversity, just like they taught us. I even remembered to read the guy his rights before the squad car got there."

Recalling the thin, frightened child who'd started the academy, Ty realized MacGregor had gone through quite a transformation. He was about to ask how long she would be in the hospital, when she looked past him, and a wide smile broke on her face.

Aware of the warmth, the traces of awe in MacGregor's expression, Ty had an intuitive flash about who her visitor was. He turned, his heart beating oddly, and saw Kate Madigan standing in the doorway.

"Hi, Sarge," he said quietly.

She was halted on the threshold, her hand touching the doorjamb as though she'd been caught off guard and needed to get her balance.

The room went silent for a moment. Even MacGregor hushed as Kate fingered the collar of her polo shirt and met Ty's gaze. "I didn't expect to see you here," she said.

She looked a little disheveled, as though she'd thrown on whatever she could find in her haste, which in this case were white jeans and the pale pink shirt. She also looked beautiful.

"I didn't expect to be here," he answered. God, how he loved that little glint of apprehension in her eyes, that uncompromising tilt to her chin. It made him want to soothe and subdue her at the same time. Kate Madigan brought out the worst and the best in him and he knew it. He even liked her rigidity. She was all sharp edges and soft spots, one of the most complicated women he'd ever met.

"Sergeant Madigan?" Melissa finally ventured.

"Oh—I'm sorry. *Melissa*, how are you?" Kate said, stepping into the room.

Ty moved aside and waved Kate toward the bed, watching as she skirted past him. I don't bite, he wanted to tell her. But then again, he thought, considering how beautiful she looked at the moment, maybe I do. He felt a warming surge of energy in his groin. He wanted to get this woman alone somewhere, *anywhere*. Listening in on his own thoughts, he smiled dryly. He also wanted to end world hunger, and he probably had about as much chance of accomplishing that.

"I'm fine," Melissa assured Kate, happily launching into her recap of the robbery attempt. Listening intently, Kate sat on the edge of the bed, and as she laughed in astonishment and pressed Melissa for details, Ty realized she *was* capable of letting down. When she trusts enough, he determined silently. Obviously she was sufficiently comfortable with MacGregor to shed the woman-in-charge image. They seemed to have the natural rapport of two girlfriends. He was also aware that Kate was pretty much ignoring him. That was okay. *For now.*

Leaving them to talk, he walked to the room's window and stared out at the street traffic three stories below. Superficially his mind was on his study, and why he seemed to have lost enthusiasm for it since his stint in the reserve officer training. On a deeper level, his thoughts were on his former D.I.—and what he was going to do about her.

Melissa's voice broke through his reflections. "Raphaell? Sergeant Madigan asked you a question."

"I asked how you'd been," Kate said as he turned to look at her.

How have I been? he wondered. "I get by," he said, remembering her answer that first night at Mother's. She remembered it, too, and her eyes narrowed a little, though not in annoyance, he decided. She was closer to smiling.

A nurse popped in at that moment to bring Melissa some medication, and to inform both Kate and Ty that visiting hours were over.

Rising to leave, Kate promised to come back and see Melissa the next day. "In the meantime, is there anything you need?" she asked.

"*Yes*," Melissa exclaimed, "a hamburger, french fries and a chocolate shake!"

"Consider it done," Ty said, laughing. "We'll have it sent up from the coffee shop next door."

Moments later, on their way down in the elevator, Ty mentioned the absence of Melissa's family members at the hospital.

"She was raised in foster homes," Kate explained. "I don't think she has anyone she calls family." The compassion in her voice told Ty how emotionally attached she'd become to the young woman. The lady cop *does* have a soft heart, he thought, smiling to himself.

The coffee shop was nearly empty as Kate and Ty entered. He ordered Melissa's food, and then turned to Kate. "How about something for you? Did you have lunch?"

"I didn't, no, but that's okay," she said. "I'm not hungry."

"Coffee, then?"

By the way she stepped back from the counter and folded her arms, Ty could see that this was a big decision for her. "I'm not a recruit anymore," he reminded her, "if that's what's stopping you. Out here in the real world they don't have no-fraternization rules."

Kate tapped her fingers slowly on her folded arms. He was a dead eye at more than darts, she thought. He had hit on *exactly* what was stopping her. There weren't any nice, neat rules to follow now, and no one knew that better than she did. They could have coffee, and anything else they chose to have. They could dance all night or run naked in the rain, and the mere possibility of either struck fear in her heart. She wasn't used to this kind of freedom, and she wasn't at all sure she liked it.

"What do I have to do?" He laughed. "Whip you at darts to get you to have a cup of coffee with me?"

"You didn't *whip* me," she said, her chin lifting automatically.

Smiling wisely, he ordered two cups of coffee and led her to a table.

"You squeaked by me, Raphaell," she insisted as they sat down. "You got lucky."

He raised a hand. "It shall go down in the annals of dart history that I squeaked by you, okay? Now do me favor. Don't call me Raphaell anymore. The name's Ty."

A waitress appeared and set stoneware cups of steaming black coffee in front of them.

Kate turned the cup in its saucer as the woman bustled away. "Ty," she said, trying the name out, liking the feel of it. She looked up, irresistibly smiling as soon as she saw his eyes, which just happened to be warm and dancing with sympathetic amusement. "Why is this so awkward, Ty?"

"I think it's because we've got this thing for each other."

"What?" Breathing out startled laughter, Kate reconsidered her coffee. It looked much too hot to drink. "You're *bad*," she said, shaking her head.

He didn't respond right away. Instead, he tore open a packet of sugar, tapped out a white stream of it into his cup and stirred it slowly. "But that's what you want, isn't it?" He set down the spoon and looked up at her. "A bad boy who'll muss up your hair a little, your clothes, maybe even your life?'' His voice dropped lower, and became slightly sandy. "Isn't that what you want?"

Kate's fingertips whitened against the cup. God, he read her too well. She took a sip of the coffee and found it scalding hot and strong. She also found it delicious. "Raphaell—*Ty*," she said, "I'm not sure we've got the timing right on this coffee date. It feels too soon, doesn't it? Maybe we should give the academy thing some time to wear off."

"How much time?"

"A year? Two? Okay, I'm kidding," she said, as he narrowed his eyes. "How about a week? Call me in a week."

He pushed his coffee cup away. "I've got a better idea. There will be no more talk about mussing up your hair, you have my word. Let's go to the pier, walk in the wind with the sea gulls, discuss world affairs. How's that sound?"

She hesitated, fascinated by the tracings of a smile on his lips, the same slow, wanton smile that made her insides want to shrink up like curling ribbon.

"Come on, Sarge," he said, "give it a chance. I can be a good boy when I have to. I was O.R., wasn't I?"

The Santa Monica pier was only fifteen minutes away from the hospital, and by the time they got there, the afternoon winds were whipping the weather flags wildly. The air smelled brisk and briny, and the clouds were thin stratus layers low in the slate sky. Shivering, Kate realized she hadn't worn a coat.

"Here," he said, pulling off his leather jacket and wrapping it around her. "Wear this."

They strolled the pier, ate hot dogs, drank lemon Cokes and watched surfers wipe out in the heavy seas. When the wind died down, they walked some more; she, lost in his black jacket, he with his hands tucked into the pockets of his jeans; both of them exquisitely sensitive to those moments when they accidentally brushed arms, or interrupted one another, or caught each other stealing a glance. They noticed the other couples walking hand in hand, the entwined forms embracing in the shadows of the pier.

It was early spring at the beach. It was falling in love time.

Soon the sun began to drop through the clouds, fringing the sky with silver fire. Ty and Kate watched the spectacle, rapt, their laughter coming quickly and a little breathlessly, their conversation seeming to flow from some similar inner source. They talked about their favorite restaurants, the old movies they loved, their childhood adventures. Ty told her about his former law practice, his maverick tactics in court, his desire to do something meaningful with his life. Kate was more reticent, but finally she confessed that her life, too, seemed off course at the moment. They discussed everything *but* world affairs, and finally they wound up on the beach, huddled on a hillock of sand, the wind in their faces, the foaming sea at their feet.

"Ever been seriously in love?" Ty threw out casually.

"I was engaged once," Kate said, "to a policeman. He was killed."

He came around slowly. "I'm sorry—"

"No, it's okay," she said quickly, as though to dismiss the subject. "It happened six years ago."

"I'm a good listener," Ty said quietly. "If you want to talk about it."

Kate hesitated, feeling her own instinctive resistance, and yet aware on some level that she *did* want to talk about it. Watching a wave roll up to their feet and recede, she felt a certain detachment come over her. When she did take a breath and begin finally, it was almost as though she was talking about someone else's tragedy. Staring out to sea, she recounted how Glenn had been cut down by a sniper's random bullet in his first year of duty, how it felt to have her life shatter, her dreams evaporate.

"That explains the sadness," he said, when she'd finished.

"What sadness?"

"In your eyes."

Another wave crested and broke, fringing the beach with white lace. "Do you still love him?" he asked.

To Kate's surprise the answer came to her almost immediately, but she held off saying it for a moment. "No," she said, "I don't think so." She supposed she would always be in love with Glenn, but not the way Ty meant, not anymore. "Sometimes I can hardly remember what it was like with him and me."

His relief was audible. "God, I'm glad you said that." He brought her face around and stared at her with eyes that she remembered vividly from her dreams. They penetrated her defenses, pierced right through her body. Finally he dropped a kiss on her mouth and breathed out warmth and frustration. "I've just about hit my limit with being good, Kate. I need to be alone with you somewhere."

She quelled the inner shudder of alarm, the instinctive need to retreat. Reaching up, touching his face, she drew her fingers down to the rough satin of his mouth, and felt a wrench of pleasure deep inside her. When he looked at her that way she didn't know what was good or bad. She just needed to be with him, too.

"Come with me to my place," he said.

"I live ten minutes away," she told him.

Smiling, still staring into her eyes, he took her hand and pulled her to her feet. They ran through the sand toward the parking lot, and when they reached Ty's Aston Martin, he swung her into his arms and pressed her up against the side of the car. "I know why they call you Storm," he said, his breath rushing over her face.

"Why?" She laughed, but the low grip in his voice caught at her senses, snared them like netting.

"Later," he promised huskily. "Let me see if I'm right, first."

He helped her into the car, let himself in and jolted the engine awake with a twist of the ignition. Steel-belted tires squealed out a protest as he pulled out of the lot and into the street traffic. Minutes into the short trip, he took her hand and curled it over the stick shift, covering it with his own. When he popped the sports car into a higher gear, she felt the vibrations shoot up her arm, felt the heat of his skin and the powerful forward surge of the car.

Nerves sparkled in her stomach. The same delicious *ching* of apprehension she'd felt before. She loved the feeling, but it frightened her. She wanted to be with him, but that frightened her, too. It was a beautiful fear that sensitized her nerves and heightened her perceptions to a clarity that was almost painful. She felt as though she could hear his breathing, count his heartbeats, eavesdrop on his private thoughts. It was exhilarating—and far too stimulating for an Irish girl from Boston. If Kate could have stopped the world at that moment, halted the car and made a run for it, she would have.

But then the acute sensitivity passed, and she was once again a mortal woman attracted to a man who totally intrigued and occasionally panicked her, a woman with a stitching pulse.

They made the trip to her place quickly, but when he pulled into her driveway he settled back in the seat and let the car idle. "One of these days," he said, gazing out the front windshield, "I'm going to have to tell you why I really took the reserve training."

Kate stared at his profile and caught a glimpse of something beneath the surface, deeper, darker. "Not now," she said, sensing instinctively that whatever he had to tell her would change things between them. "Don't tell me now."

She let herself out of his car and dashed for her apartment door, laughing nervously as she unlocked it and entered the shadows of the living room. She patted along the wall for the light switch.

"Don't turn it on," he said, coming up behind her, covering her hand.

Kate heard him kick the door shut, and her heart went silent in the still, dark room. She dropped her head, breathing deeply...and gasped as he swung her around and pressed her to the wall.

"I want Kate Madigan this way," he said under his breath, "in the darkness, with the moonlight streaming through the windows. I want to be the man to muss up her hair and her clothes and her life."

He began with her hair, working his fingers into its auburn weight, lifting its heaviness away from her face. Cool air fanned her throat seconds before he kissed it, his lips a fiery sweetness along her skin.

Aware of his other hand pressed to her thigh, Kate went rigid as he began to bring it slowly up her body, his fingers caressing the line of her hip, the heel of his palm nestling into the curve of her pelvis.

She arched up with a soft gasp as he slipped his hand under her polo shirt. The heat of his bare skin against hers was a dizzying shock to her senses. "Oh, not *there*," she pleaded as he moved his hand to the underswell of her breast and cradled it, lifting its weight in his palm.

"Why not here?" he asked. "God, I love you here. You're warm and soft. You're alive in my hand."

Her stomach muscles tautened as he encircled the aureole of her nipple with his thumb and his fingers bit gently into her flesh, caressing her through her filmy bra. Deep strokes of pleasure pierced her. "Ah, it almost hurts," she gasped.

"Hurts?" He murmured the word gently, riveting every nerve in her body. "Do you have any idea how much I want to touch you this way—and if it hurts a little, then *yes*, that, too." Releasing her, he gathered her into his arms and kissed her hair, a soft rage in his words. "Do you know that you're tender as a baby? I knew you'd be like this. I knew you'd cry and quiver and be sweeter than any woman should ever be. I wanted to take it slow, arouse you inch by beautiful inch, but I'm not doing a very good job of that, am I?"

Limp against his body, she breathed, "If you do any better a job, I'll lose my mind."

She let herself be held, rocked, crushed by him fiercely. It was good in his arms, it was heaven and hell. Cradled in his strength, she could feel the gradual erosion of her resistance. She was melting under his heat, her rigid muscles softening against him. And yet, oddly, as her resistance drained away, her senses sharpened again, thrilling to his scent, his muscled hardness.

Yes, it was good in his arms...

She sighed inwardly, a nerve-spun sound that floated like strands of silk through her body, and then she nuzzled into the caressing stroke of his hand in her hair. She was a kitten arching up to meet a warm touch. She was a woman pleasuring to a man's hands, *good hands*. The sharpness of it all, the sweetness was more than she could bear. Was she supposed to feel this way, to want something this much?

Was she breaking the rules again?

He pressed his palm against the delicate curvature of her spine, and slowly slid his hand down her back to settle on the tiny, taut mound at the base of her spine.

Kate's heart flared, a fiery tenderness inside her. She pulled back, looking up at him.

"Amazing," he said, laughter shimmering. "I love to touch you this way and watch what happens to your eyes. The pupils shrink with doubt... and then they dilate and darken and get huge with excitement."

"Don't say things like that, Ty," she pleaded, her voice a ragged, sexy whisper. "Don't talk to me like that—and that's an order."

"An order? Then how about if I talk to you like this?" Staring into the depths of her eyes, he unsnapped her jeans and eased his hands inside the waistband. "We're going to make love, Sergeant Madigan, here against the wall, there on the floor, in the kitchen on a chair and, finally, *maybe* in the bedroom." He sank his hands deeper and took hold of her hip bones. "I want you, any way, *anywhere* I can get you."

The sound that slipped from Kate's throat was a soft, shocked whimper. It was the tiny, sharp cry of a female animal calling her mate. It was the sweet, strangled longing of a woman who'd held on and held back too long.

"Do you know what you're doing to me?" he said, breathing the words through his teeth. Bending, he hooked an arm under her knees and lifted her into his arms. "No walls, no floors," he said, "the bedroom first. I want you in bed, lying next to me, stretched out underneath me, curled around me."

Kate's bedroom shimmered with the soft, golden light of the bedside lamp she always left on. As he carried her into a room that was newly feminine and lowered her onto a bed covered with eyelet pillows, he reached to turn the light off, then hesitated. "No," he said huskily, "I want to see you."

He sat next to her on the bed and slipped his hands underneath the soft cotton fabric, easing it up until her lacy bra was exposed. "I want to watch the storm break inside you," he said, cupping the fullness of her breasts in his hands, lifting her to him.

Kate arched up, a gasp in her throat. His mouth was sensual and tantalizing. His kisses were sweet torture as he played with her lips, sipping and teasing and murmuring, denying her the deep, thrilling kiss she wanted. His tongue delved at the crease of her lips, entrancing her, driving her wild, until finally she dug her fingers into his back and whispered, "*Harder*, kiss me harder."

"Like this?" he asked, cupping the back of her head and moving his mouth over hers with a pressure that was hard and undeniably sexual in its demand. Forcing her lips open with his tongue, he filled her mouth with deep, thrilling strokes of pleasure.

Yes, like that, she moaned inwardly as he lowered her onto the bed.

He moved alongside her, easing his body next to hers. "Another surprise," he said huskily, pulling one of the pillows out from under her head and tossing it aside. "I wouldn't have figured you for all this frilly stuff, Sarge. I like it." Gazing down at her, holding her with his eyes, he slipped his finger under the delicate front fastening of her bra and lifted it, coaxing the closure apart. "But what I'm going to like even better is you *without* all this frilly stuff."

Nervous laughter trembled in Kate's throat. Impulsively, she grabbed for a pillow to cover herself. "Uh-uh," she said, holding the eyelet ruffles to her chest, "you first."

"You *do* love a contest, don't you, Madigan?" Laughing, he caught a corner of the pillow, and they tugged for a moment before he wrested it away from her and sent it flying. The light flickered wildly behind him as the pillow grazed the lamp and knocked something off the nightstand, a small object that hit the hardwood floor with a sharp crackling sound.

Oblivious, Ty twined his fingers through her hair, cradling her, lifting her. Kate rose to meet his kiss, and only then did it begin to register that she'd heard something crash to the floor. The echo of shattered glass brought her up on an elbow.

"Leave it, whatever it is," Ty whispered. "We'll get it later."

But Kate couldn't leave it. A flash of insight told her what had broken. "Wait," she said, staying him with her hand. "*Wait*, Ty."

"What's wrong?" He searched her face.

A sudden sense of urgency impelled her, stiffening her movements as she tried to straighten her clothing. "Please, I have to get up."

"Kate, what—"

"Ty, *please*, let me up."

He swung his legs off the bed and offered her a hand.

"No," Kate whispered, moving around him to the edge of the bed where she saw the tiny golden picture frame facedown on the floor. With a soft moan, she slid off the bed, crouched and picked it up, turning it over, staring at its splintered surface.

"What is it?" Ty asked, and then his voice changed. "Is it Glenn?"

The edge to his question, the low hoarseness was painful for Kate to hear. "Yes," she said, "the two of us, at our engagement party."

"May I see it?"

She handed it to him slowly, a terrible constriction in her throat.

He stared at it a moment, one of his thumbs working along the edge of the gilt frame. "I don't know what I'm supposed to say. The usual things? Nice-looking couple—"

"Don't," she said, reaching for the picture, pulling it out of his hands. "Don't say anything." Glancing down at the broken glass, at Glenn's distorted features, Kate flinched as though the picture were shattering all over again. Suddenly the tightness in her throat became something else—anxiety, pain—and a memory flickered along the edge of her mind, half-formed, demanding to be acknowledged.

"Ty, please," she said, "you have to go."

"*Go?* Why?"

She shook her head. She couldn't explain it, not to him, not even to herself. Forcing the image of Glenn from her mind, she jerked to her feet and walked to the dresser. "This isn't right," she whispered, her back to Ty. "Can't you see that?"

"Not right? What do you mean?"

"You and I. Now. *Here*. It's not right." Hearing him come up behind her, she drew into herself protectively.

"Why isn't it right, Kate?" he asked her quietly, tentatively. "You said you didn't love him anymore. You said you could hardly remember what it was like with him."

Her heart wrenched with confusion. "I know, but I'm remembering now," she said, her voice catching. "Oh, Ty, please try to understand. There's never been anyone else in the apartment, in this room, in this bed."

"Glenn is dead, Kate," Ty said bluntly. "He's been gone for six years—"

She swung around, suddenly furious at his callousness. "Yes, he's gone. Yes, he's dead—" a startled gasp tangled in her throat, and without warning a revelation surged up from inside her, a burst of damning words that rushed out before she could stop them "—and it was *my fault*."

"What?"

Kate reared back in shock. A strange sensation flared in her throat, part surprise, part horror. She caught her lower lip between her teeth reflexively, and it was several seconds before she could answer the stark question in Ty's eyes. *"I said it was my fault,"* she whispered, admitting it aloud for the first time. She stared at him, stricken.

"What do you mean it was your fault?" He took hold of her shoulders.

A hidden pocket of pain welled up in Kate, a legacy of the tragedy she'd forced out of her consciousness years ago. Jolted back into her awareness, the memory rushed at her like a gathering storm.

"Tell me, Kate," Ty insisted.

She nodded her head, trying to calm the tumult inside her.

"I was a rookie with the La Mesa police," she told him at last, her voice halting. "My partner and I had been assigned to an assault case, a teenage girl who'd been beaten up by a neighborhood gang. God, it was pathetic what they'd done to her. I wanted to go back, follow up on the case, but my partner wouldn't do it."

She pulled away from Ty and sat on the edge of the bed, still clutching the picture. "I remember telling Glenn that night that I was going anyway, *alone* if I had to. We argued about it, a terrible argument. He said it was too dangerous, and finally—to stop me from going, I suppose—he went himself."

She looked up at Ty, anguish welling up in her chest. "He was shot that night, a sniper's bullet. The woman lived in a gang-infested area, a war zone. Oh God," she groaned softly, shaking her head, "if only I hadn't fought with him . . . If only I'd been able to stop him."

She felt tears burning her throat.

"Kate," Ty breathed, "have you been carrying that around with you for six years?"

Had she? She shook her head in confusion. She'd had terrible, incapacitating guilt for days, but then, after the memorial service, she hadn't allowed herself to think about the circumstances of Glenn's death anymore. She'd forced it from her mind, telling herself it did no good to dwell on things that couldn't be undone. Later that same year, she'd made a decision. She would do what Glenn had always wanted to do, become a D.I. She took a deep breath and released it. Was that her atonement, she wondered, keeping his dream alive?

"Kate," Ty was saying, "you aren't responsible. The sniper was going to kill *someone* that night. If it hadn't been

Glenn it would have been the next man, the next woman, the next child that came by. It could have been *you*."

She shook her head, confused. Behind her eyes, she saw a tiny jagged streak of red lightning. Through the impending headache, she could hear Ty telling her that she'd been letting the incident control her life, that on some level she was still blaming herself. The words made sense, but she couldn't integrate them emotionally. She couldn't deal with blame now.

"Ty, I'm sorry," she said, turning to him, a whispered entreaty in her voice. "Please . . . I need to be alone now."

He stared at her for a long moment, concern and frustration clouding his features. "All right," he said finally, "I'll go, but I want to know when I can see you again."

She shook her head, pain throbbing behind her eye. "I don't know. I need some time . . . to sort things out."

"I've got time," he said quietly. With that he turned and walked to the door, hesitating a moment at the threshold. When he spoke his voice was gentle, sad. "I can compete with flesh and blood men, Kate, but I can't compete with ghosts. They live forever."

As he disappeared through the door, Kate sat on the bed, dry-eyed, staring at the picture in her hands, the shards of glass on the floor.

Chapter Eleven

When Kate arrived at Melissa's hospital room the next day, she found the patient poring over anatomy and physiology textbooks.

"The bullet splintered the styloid on my second metatarsal," Melissa informed Kate succinctly, waving her over to look at a color illustration of the bones of the foot. "See, it passed right between the first metatarsal and the second metatarsal, exited my foot here and lodged in Mini-Mart's floor. Nifty, huh?"

Kate quelled a smile. "I'm impressed, MacGregor," she said, glancing around at the array of books on Melissa's bed. "Are you consulting on your own case?"

Melissa quirked an eyebrow. "You got that right. They're not too sharp here, Sergeant Madigan. One of the orderlies came in last night and threw a sheet over my head. Got me confused with the coronary thrombosis case next door. That man was one hundred and six years old."

"The orderly?" Kate asked, astounded.

"No, the deceased."

"Oh . . . of course."

"I could have been a medical anomaly by now," Mac-Gregor said, nodding earnestly.

"Sounds like a close call," Kate commiserated, giving in to a wry smile.

Melissa didn't seem to notice. "Don't worry. I'm on my toes," she said, and then glanced at her foot. "Well—you know what I mean."

Kate laughed softly. "I know exactly what you mean." Hearing her own laughter, Kate reflected on how bleak things had looked when she'd awakened that morning, the despair she'd felt. It was remarkable how her doldrums had lightened after just a few minutes with MacGregor. "When are they letting you out of here?" she asked.

"Soon as the swelling goes down they're going to cast my foot. Then they'll spring me."

"Well, let me know if you need anything," Kate offered, "like a ride home, maybe some help around the house?"

"Thanks, but I'll be okay," Melissa assured her, settling back in the pillows as though her independence was a point of pride. The young woman obviously had every intention of fending for herself, Kate realized, deciding not to press any further assistance on her unless she asked for help.

"What is it?" Kate questioned, aware that Melissa was scrutinizing her. "Is my lipstick smeared?"

"You look a little under the weather today, Sergeant Madigan," she said. "Anything wrong?"

Kate sighed deeply. *"Everything."* She was surprised at how easily the admission came. "Everything's wrong, Melissa. And please call me Kate."

"Sit down, Kate," Melissa insisted, patting her bed, "and let 'er rip. I'm a good listener."

Kate pushed an anatomy book aside and sat, but she didn't let 'er rip. "Thanks, but it's too complicated," she said, turning to stare out the window and sinking into silence. "What's it all about?" she asked after a moment, addressing her question to the window. "Is life supposed to be a struggle? An uphill fight?"

Sighing in frustration, she turned to her former recruit in search of wisdom. "Are we supposed to be happy in this life, Melissa? Even if we've made mistakes?"

"Everybody makes mistakes, don't they?"

"Yes, but this one had . . . terrible consequences."

"Umm, sounds heavy," Melissa observed reflectively. After a moment, she pursed her lips and tapped them briefly. "I guess it all boils down to your intentions, doesn't it? If you've got it in mind to do something wrong, to hurt someone, let's say. Well, that's one thing. If you hurt them without meaning to, that's another."

"I didn't intend to hurt anyone," Kate said quietly.

"Well then, that's all that matters, isn't it?" Melissa shrugged as though the issue was settled.

"Is it that easy?" Kate looked up, hoping it was. She stared into Melissa's eyes, thinking that her former recruit had the face of a child and the gaze of an old soul. In the wake of that thought, a childhood memory began to coalesce in Kate's mind . . . she'd been ten years old, falsely accused of an act of vandalism. She'd indignantly denied it to the school officials and to the police, but she'd had no proof of her whereabouts, no alibi. They'd let her go finally, but she'd never known if they believed her. *Proof won't make you innocent, Kate*, her mother had told her. *It doesn't matter what they believe. If you're right with your heart, that's enough.*

Intellectually, Kate knew that Ty was right. She wasn't to blame for what had happened to Glenn. She supposed she'd always known it. But now Melissa had hit on the deeper issue, which Kate had never faced. Her own intentions. She hadn't meant to hurt Glenn, not that tragic night six years ago, not ever. She knew that without a shadow of a doubt, and the awareness brought her a cleansing sense of relief. She'd begged Glenn not to go that night, and yet she, herself, would have gone in a minute if he hadn't intervened. She'd cared more for his safety than for her own.

Kate came out of the recollection smiling at Melissa's matter-of-fact expression. "How'd you get so smart?" she said.

Melissa tapped a glass pitcher sitting on the stainless steel tray next to the bed. "Must be the hospital water."

Kate laughed. "I'll be sure to stop at the drinking fountain on my way out." She picked up one of the anatomy books and leafed through it. "Are you really going to read all these?"

"I've read half of them already," Melissa informed her. "Actually I'm killing two birds with one stone. I'm researching my own case, of course, but I'm also studying up for when I take an anatomy class. I've decided to become a homicide detective."

"Homicide?" Kate half gasped, half laughed. "You don't go halfway on anything, do you, MacGregor?"

She lifted a shoulder. "I live to solve crimes."

Kate smiled, but Melissa's simple statement of purpose brought her in touch with traces of an emotion she hadn't felt in years. Envy. Given her own achievements, it took her a moment to figure out why she should envy Melissa—and then she realized it had nothing to do with achievement. It had to do with trusting oneself. Melissa wanted something and she was going after it. It didn't matter that other people thought she couldn't or shouldn't do it. She wasn't doing it for anyone but herself. She had nothing to prove. Her reasons were pure. Kate admired that more than she could say.

"Homicide," Kate murmured. "I can see it now. You'll wear a crumpled trench coat and carry a magnifying glass. You'll be faintly supercilious but always polite."

"I'll drive the suspect crazy with my probing questions and my brilliant deductive reasoning," Melissa chimed in.

Kate swung around, addressing the window again. "Watch out, criminal minds. Pacific Police Academy has spawned a female Sherlock Holmes."

They both laughed, warmth and a new comradeship in their smiles. Moments later, as Kate stood to go, she felt a tug of wistfulness for her own lost opportunity. Melissa's enthusiasm always seemed to remind her that she'd once wanted to be a detective, too.

"I don't have to wish you luck, Melissa," she said. "You make your own luck." She caught the young woman's hand and squeezed it. "Stay in touch or I'll have you arrested, hear? And I meant that about calling me if you needed anything."

"I will," Melissa said, squeezing Kate's hand back.

Kate was on her way out the door when Melissa called out a thank-you for the hamburger and shake. "Scrumptious," she said, grinning. "I thanked Ty this morning when he stopped in to say goodbye."

"Goodbye?" Kate swung around, alarmed. "What does that mean?"

"He said he was going away for a while," Melissa explained, "but he didn't seem to want to talk about it. I thought he might have said something to you."

"No," Kate said, her heart going silent. "He didn't say anything."

Kate was pulled over for speeding on the way home from the hospital.

"Sergeant Madigan?!" gasped the young traffic cop as he peered at her through the open window of her car.

Kate immediately recognized him as a recruit she'd had two years before. He'd barely squeaked through academically, but he'd seemed a dedicated, decent sort. She'd always wondered what kind of a police officer he would make.

"Sorry, ma'am, but you were doing forty-five in a thirty-five zone."

She stared at him hard. "Do you like what you're doing, Gallagher?"

"Writing you up, ma'am?"

"No, I mean police work, Gallagher. Are you happy?"

He blinked several times. "No, ma'am, I guess not. Not really."

"Then stop doing it, Gallagher," she said earnestly. "Don't waste another minute of your life doing something that doesn't give you joy."

"Ma'am?"

Kate could see she'd thrown him a curve. She wasn't sure herself where that speech had come from, but she liked the sound of it. Now, if she could just get home in time to telephone Ty before he left... for wherever.

When she reached her apartment, she realized she didn't have Ty's telephone number. It was in his file at the academy! She tried information but they had no listing for him, and then she called the academy on the chance that someone might be in on a Sunday—odder things have been known to happen—but she didn't connect. "Well." She sighed, hanging up the phone and picking up her car keys. "I guess this means another speeding ticket."

She spotted a black-and-white in the oncoming traffic as she roared down Pacific Coast Highway toward the academy. Letting up on the gas, she sailed past it and breathed a sigh of relief as the officer honked and waved at her. Thank you, Gallagher, she thought, smiling.

It was only as she sat down at her desk and picked up the telephone that she hesitated. What was she going to say to Ty if he answered? She could mention that she'd heard he was going away. That would start the conversation...

Her stomach knotted with tension as his phone rang repeatedly. He wasn't going to answer. He'd already gone. As she replaced the receiver and sank forward on her elbows, she told herself it had all been premature anyway. She didn't know what she was going to say to him, and until she did she had no business calling him. If she got together with him impulsively, without thinking it through, there would be more fiascoes like the night before. No, she couldn't contact him until she was ready to let herself become involved.

Involved? She shook her head at that loaded word. The very thought of becoming involved with anyone—especially a man like Ty Raphaell—was still slightly terrifying to her for some reason. Maybe she'd been alone too long. Maybe she was no longer capable of having a relationship.

A heaviness pressed down on her as she settled back in her chair and swung around slowly, staring at the commendations and awards on her walls. She'd achieved a great deal in her five years as a drill instructor and she was proud of all of it, but what did it really mean? she wondered.

The office seemed smaller to her for some reason, and confining in a way she didn't understand. The plaques symbolized the success and recognition she'd been striving for, sacrificing for, but that recognition felt oddly empty now, as though onionskin scrolls and calligraphic words were all she had to show for her efforts.

She knew that wasn't true. She'd trained some fine officers . . . and yet something was missing. She knew what that was where her heart was concerned. It was a man named Ty Raphaell. Confused and dispirited, she rose and walked to the window, staring out, standing in a shaft of sunlight for several moments before the truth of her deliberations came to her. She was frightened, flat-out scared. Ty wanted her, physically, emotionally, the whole package. And as much as she wanted him, that package had her panicked. Before she could ever hope to find the courage to deal with Ty, she had to deal with herself. Ask the hard questions. Who was Kate Madigan? What did she want? She'd accomplished many things in her life, all of them noteworthy, but they weren't *hers*. She'd set her own goals aside and become a D.I. because Glenn had wanted to be one. She'd embraced her grandfather's work ethic in adeath grip trying to be the kind of Madigan he would have approved of, bless his Irish police captain heart.

A bittersweet sigh of sudden insight filled her. She'd listened too well to the voices of loved ones in her head, to the guilt in her heart. Kate Madigan had been so busy honoring other people's dreams and expectations, she'd forgotten to honor her own.

Turning around, taking in the plaques and awards again, she made a decision. Come tomorrow, she promised herself, there would be some changes made.

Kate had all night to consider her decision, and by the next morning, the first day of the new session at the academy, she was even more firm in her resolve. She arrived at work early, went straight to Art Buchanan's office, and was surprised to find the dean with him.

"Sergeant Madigan?" Buchanan said, waving her in. "We were just talking about you."

Kate's heart beat heavily in her chest. She hadn't planned to make her speech in front of the dean, but she supposed it couldn't be helped. Entering the room, she nodded to them both. "Art, Dean Hogan, I'd like to—"

"Hold it, Kate," Buchanan said, standing. "We've got some news for you."

"News?"

"Yes, Kate." Dean Hogan's deep bass voice rumbled around the small office like thunder. "We've finally come to a decision about filling Art's position, Kate, and I'm happy to say that you are our unanimous choice."

Looking from one man to the other, Kate mouthed the words, "Me? You're offering *me* the executive training adviser position?"

"We most certainly are," Hogan assured her. "And we'd like to announce it at the orientation session today, with the new recruits and their families present."

Kate shook her head, dazed. Not in her wildest dreams had she expected this. "I'm sorry, sir," she said, meeting

Dean Hogan's benevolent smile, "but I can't possibly accept. I've decided to go back on active duty. I'm going to become a detective."

Kate's decision rolled through the academy like a shock wave. The brass held meetings, urged her to reconsider and finally offered a raise in pay, but Kate held fast. Even her new crop of recruits applied some pressure. They wanted to be trained by the legendary Screamin' Blue Meanie. Before the week was out, everyone but Tommy had tried to talk her out of it. His reaction had been a laconic grin and a mumbled, "Way to go, Storm."

With a tremendous amount of work ahead of her before she could even apply for a detective position, Kate began to make her plans. To be competitive, she would need specific knowledge in the area of her specialty, and since she'd chosen fraud she had several tough college courses to get through, including business and contract law. All the preparation kept her from the other much tougher decision regarding Ty. One step at a time, she told herself.

One of the academy secretaries offered to do the legwork in getting Kate enrolled at a local college, and when the first night of classes arrived she found herself wandering around the huge campus, trying to decipher a map of the grounds by moonlight.

She finally found the business law class tucked away in a corner of the fine arts building. The logic of that placement escaped her but she wasn't there to question why, as the saying went. She entered quietly and sat in the back of the crowded classroom, arranging her books and glancing around at the other students. For the most part they looked *young*, late teens, early twenties at most. Could a woman pushing thirty compete with the best and the brightest? she wondered, feeling a trace of nervousness set in. She'd been the teacher for so many years that student status was going to take some getting used to.

She was jotting the date in her notebook when the door
wung open behind her and the instructor strode in. Jolted
vith disbelief, Kate watched him walk to the front of the
oom. As he pivoted, set his books down on the lectern and
ooked up at the class, Kate pressed back against her chair.
t was *Ty Raphaell*!

She immediately sank down and began rifling through her
1otebook, looking for the class schedule she'd received from
he college. She knew she hadn't seen Raphaell's name when
she'd signed up for the class! She found it finally, her heart
1ammering as she thumbed through the pages to the *B*s. She
spotted the problem instantly. There were several business
aw classes scheduled, with various dates, times and loca-
ions, but under the heading, Instructor, a single word was
isted: Staff.

Staff? She groaned inwardly and crept back up to a sit-
ing position. What a sneaky thing for the college to do!
Peeking around the spiky bouffant hairdo of the young
woman in front of her, Kate checked again to make sure her
eyes hadn't deceived her.

They hadn't. Her instructor was introducing himself to
he class in his easy, offhandedly sexy manner, smiling the
way only he could smile, and generally riveting every female in the room. He was wearing denim jeans and a jacket,
and the polo shirt underneath was nearly as green as his
eyes. *Oh, yes,* she thought, a nervous sigh on her lips, that
definitely *was* Ty Raphaell up there.

Kate took a steadying breath. He hadn't seen her yet, but
she prepared herself for the moment, flexing her shoulders,
ilting her head with polite interest. She was going to be cool
f it killed her. After that first call, she hadn't intended to
contact him again until she knew her own mind where he
was concerned, but here she was. *His student!* There was
some kind of awful irony in that, but Kate wasn't about to
et herself get mired in concepts like poetic justice.

He began his lecture, and it was immediately apparent that he wasn't going to take a traditional approach. Watching him, riveted, Kate gradually eased her way, desk and all, out from behind the cover of the bouffant hairdo.

"There are no rules in this class," he told them, sitting on the edge of the table, his arms folded. "I give exams because the school won't pay me if I don't. The only thing I require of you is intellectual curiosity. When I engage you in a dialogue, I want to feel you there, behind the words. It's not enough that I challenge you to think. That's my job. I want you to challenge back." He glanced around the room, looking at each of them. "Put me to the test," he said, his gaze finally colliding with Kate's.

She steeled herself as he focused in on her, his eyes narrowing. "Surprise me," he added under his breath.

Kate stared at him, unable to move. Her heart was beating in every cell of her body, even in the fingertips of the hand she'd curled around her felt-tip pen. God, she thought, what am I *doing* here?

Long after he'd reluctantly broken their eye contact and gone back to addressing the class, Kate was still sitting there stunned. His lecture had something to do with legal rights and the students were following it raptly, but for the life of her Kate couldn't track the content. Her brain was the consistency of a three-minute egg! She did have the presence of mind to figure out one thing though: *he was going to be tough.*

He paced the room when he talked, and he had the kind of brilliant, restless mind that she suspected wouldn't suffer intellectual laziness kindly. Even more disconcerting, he had a way of stopping abruptly and throwing out a provocative question to whomever happened to be in his line of sight.

Finally it was Kate's turn. "You in the back? Yes," he said as she pointed to herself. "How do you think legal rights might be defined?"

"Defined?" Kate gathered her wits. "Do you mean our right to property, to free speech?"

"No," he said brusquely, "I'm talking about defining, appropriating and protecting those rights. How do you think that might be done? By force, for instance? Logic? Tradition?"

"Probably by some combination of all three?" she hazarded.

"An interesting hedge, Ms.—"

"Madigan."

"*Madigan.*" His tone was reflective, ironical. He was savoring not only her name, but his position of superiority over her, Kate decided, bridling a little.

"That was a safe answer, Ms. Madigan," he informed her, "but not necessarily a smart one. Do you really think *force* should be used, for example? Would you have us reverting to caveman tactics? Hitting each other over the head with clubs?"

"I didn't have clubs in mind," she said, meeting his amused gaze levelly, "but it would save time."

A smile flashed. "An expedient woman, I like that. One would almost think you were in some branch of the military, Ms. Madigan. Or law enforcement?"

"One *would* think that, wouldn't one?" she said archly, aware that the entire class was watching them, puzzled.

"A woman in uniform?" he murmured, brushing her with his cool, green gaze. "Works for me."

It went on that way, he thrusting, she parrying, a duel of double entendres as he used points of law to gently skewer her attitudes and opinions. It was his milieu and Kate was at a disadvantage, but she held up reasonably well. Finally he went on to other topics and other students, and she had a moment to catch her breath. It wasn't until the end of the session, when he veered off the track of legal maneuverings and brought up the question of good faith negotiations, that he turned back to her again.

"What do you think, Ms. Madigan? Is there ever a time that you should trust your fellow man? Take a risk? O should we always swathe ourselves in protective bunting and play it safe?"

"Legally speaking?" Kate asked.

He shrugged. "If you must."

By the quiet intensity of his gaze, Kate knew he wasn' talking about a legal definition of trust, he was talking about taking emotional risks, opening your heart to another person.

"I guess it would depend on who the fellow man is," she said cautiously.

"Okay, just for the sake of argument...take me."

"Take you where?" The class began to laugh, and Kate raised a hand. "Sorry," she said, "I guess the real question is *why* should I trust you?"

"Because I was a Boy Scout?"

"Hmm, and I suppose you helped little old ladies across the street and rescued cats from trees?"

He raised two fingers. "On my honor, I will help other people at all times, keep myself physically strong, mentally awake and morally straight."

A big yes on the physically strong part, Kate thought suppressing a smile. "I'm impressed," she admitted, "but anybody can recite the Boy Scouts' oath. How do I know you're telling the truth?"

"You don't," he said, holding her with his gaze. "It's beginning to look like you're just going to have to trust me, isn't it?"

Kate had no answer for that, no answer at all...

After a moment a young blond woman in the front row whispered loudly, "Hell, if she won't, *I* will."

Laughter broke out until Ty quieted the class and addressed them all, bringing up the concept of fiduciary duty. "Once you put your trust in someone," he explained, "the law imposes certain responsibilities on you, one being that you can no longer keep that person at arm's length." With a meaningful glance at Kate, he went on to explain the concept in terms of its business implications, and finally he thanked the class and dismissed them for the night.

Still slightly shell-shocked, Kate gathered her books together, watching as the students, primarily young coeds, flocked toward Ty and collected around him. Unwilling to fight through a gaggle of adoring college women—and not at all sure she was prepared for a face-to-face encounter with him—she left quickly.

He was still on her mind long after she arrived home. He'd been a potent force in that classroom, and she couldn't wipe the image from her mind. He was brash and fast and cocksure of himself, a man in his element. Power became him, she reasoned, not only because of the way he wielded it but also because he had balancing traits. He could be sensitive, he could read a woman's needs and speak to them with such tenderness.

God, how well she knew that tenderness, and how terribly she missed it. Sometimes the yearning cut into her like a knife. The only thing stopping her now was him, she realized. She had no idea how he felt about her, and she certainly didn't understand the workings of the brilliant mind behind his mesmerizing green eyes. What did he want from her? she wondered . . . if anything.

She forced herself to study as the evening wore on, and finally she put him out of her thoughts. But that night he stole into her dreams again, and she felt the full paralyzing effect of the power she'd witnessed in his class. Sweeping all her objections away, he took her with all the controlled ferocity of a warrior with tender prey. It was harrowing and stunning, and as she came out of the dream, shiny with perspiration, she could almost hear him soothing her with husky whispers and dark, erotic words.

As the second night of class neared, Kate considered transferring to another night, another teacher. She didn't,

of course. That would have been cowardly. Instead, sh
prepared herself for more of the same, and she got it. T
singled her out with provocative questions and she rose t
the challenge more often than not. They engaged in severa
spirited exchanges, and finally whenever Ty glanced Kate'
way, the class immediately hushed, waiting with rapt atten
tion and some bewilderment.

Kate assumed Ty's siege had to do with the night she ha
asked him to leave, but the hint of raffish charm in hi
manner told her there was more to it than that. This was
payback for the way she'd roughed him up as a recruit.

"What constitutes a valid contract, Ms. Madigan?" T
asked her midway through that evening's class.

Kate smiled. She'd done her homework and was ready fo
this one. "A valid contract consists of an offer, an accep
tance and an exchange of value."

"You seem to grasp the theory. Now let's see if you ca
apply it."

His first example had to do with a fairly typical busines
transaction, and Kate recognized it immediately as a vali
contract. Her explanation seemed to satisfy him.

"Okay—let's try something a little different," he sug
gested. "Say a man and a woman have a mutual interest i
each other and he wants something more tangible, what d
you suppose he ought to offer her?"

The class tittered and began to buzz.

"More tangible?" Kate questioned. "I don't under
stand."

Ty sat on the table and folded his arms. "Sure you do
Ms. Madigan. Think about it. What should he offer her?"

A nerve sparked in Kate's throat. Ignoring it, she pursed
her lips and tapped them thoughtfully. "I guess that woul
depend on what she wants."

"What do you suppose that is?"

"She probably wants to know what *he* wants."

He looked down at his folded arms contemplatively, then raised his eyes to meet hers. "He wants to dance with her again."

The husky edge in his voice enflamed Kate's imagination. *Dance?* Her fingers curled around the edge of the desk. She tried to smile, her heart beating wildly. "She accepts."

He glanced down again, his jaws flexing against a smile. "Does what we've just done constitute a valid contract, Ms. Madigan?"

"Yes . . . I think so."

The spell was broken as one of the students piped up, "No, it doesn't! Nothing of value was exchanged."

"Right, and the law doesn't recognize social contracts as enforceable," another one chimed in.

Ty nodded to the group. "You're right, but you're also wrong. Something of great value could have been exchanged. What if this dance was more than just a dance? What if it was symbolic of his deeper feelings?"

"Oh, like he's in love with her or something?"

"Or something," Ty answered quietly. He stared out at the class, and Kate waited for him to glance her way. When he did it was a brief, grazing connection, like being sideswiped by a bolt of lightning.

"So...what do you think, class?" he said. "Have we got a contract or not?"

Kate hadn't the faintest idea. She was barely aware of what happened in the class from that point on. She heard the debate waging around her, but she couldn't concentrate. It was like a radio frequency she couldn't quite hold on to.

When the class ended, Ty was swamped again. Students pelted him with questions, which he tried valiantly to field. Kate waited a while, expecting him to catch her eye, to give her some signal. When he didn't, she walked outside into the night air and started for her car. No need to wait, she thought, her heart soaring with anticipation. I'll be hearing from him. *We have a contract.*

Chapter Twelve

Surrounded by the familiar clutter of his college office, Ty Raphaell sat tilted back in his chair, his feet propped up on the desk. He had office hours scheduled for this afternoon, and he'd decided to come by early to dope out his lecture for tomorrow night's business law class. Kate Madigan's unexpected appearance had thrown the sequence of his talks off a little. *Try a lot,* he thought dryly. He wasn't even sure what was on the agenda for tomorrow night.

He also had no idea why she was taking his class, but he intended to find out. Any day now. He nodded slowly at the thought, a muscle tightening in his jaw. Talk about turning the tables! He'd been biding his time with her, partly because he hadn't yet come to a decision about his study, but mostly because he wanted to be sure she was ready before he made his move. It was obvious just by looking at her that she'd come to some decision since the last time they'd been together, but it wasn't at all clear what that decision was.

She seemed softer in some ways, more feminine somehow—and if it was possible, even more beautiful. But Kate

THE PASSIONS OF KATE MADIGAN

Madigan was never exactly what she seemed. She was also high-strung, unpredictable, skittish about involvement. Experience had taught him that. And it had taught him one more thing. You didn't rush a nervous woman. You hung back, watched and waited. You let her come to you.

Settling back, he imagined that moment, saw her standing in his doorway, her hair long and wild, her hand outstretched. It was a beguiling vision, and it brought a hot, sweet twist of anticipation to his chest. How long was it going to take her? he wondered. *How long could he hold out?*

Moments later, gazing absently at the research documents piled up next to his calfskin moccasins, he remembered the other reason he'd come in early today. He stretched forward, took one of the reports off the stack and thumbed through it, his mind on the trip he'd taken recently to revisit his old army post in the northwest. Finally, exhaling deeply, he dropped the document into the garbage can.

Ten seconds later, that same can was overflowing with documents, all of them sociological impact studies of "stress training" from various universities. After months of deliberation, Ty Raphaell had finally come to a decision.

His recent trip to the state of Washington had brought him in touch with some dark memories. The base where he'd gone through boot camp looked exactly as it had eighteen years before, as though time hadn't touched it. But the D.I. he'd trained under was long dead.

Ty no longer harbored hostility toward the man, but he felt no sympathy for him, either. He'd abused his authority, brutalized the recruits. He'd taken perverse satisfaction in breaking men as if they were wild horses, and one of the casualties had been a buddy of Ty's.

The rage Ty felt at that injustice had eaten at him for years, fueling him in later legal fights, motivating his maverick tactics in court. In a way, he supposed his unresolved

anger could have accounted for the drive that had made him
so successful, but the brutality issue had continued to haunt
him.

When he'd finally decided to do something about it, the
local police academy's program had seemed the logical place
for some firsthand research. He smiled ironically, recalling
his first few weeks at Pacific. Sergeant Madigan had almost convinced him he had a righteous cause. It wasn't until he'd fought his way through the program—and especially
after MacGregor's brush with death—that he'd begun to
appreciate the essential value of the training. It gave recruits the belief in themselves they needed to face the ter-
rors of the street. *It saved lives.*

He'd learned a lot in the eighteen weeks of recruit hell,
mostly about himself. It had taught him about lines, and
why they were drawn and how people got hurt when you
crossed them. Oddly, he'd gone into the program expecting
to witness abuses of power, and he'd come out of it realizing that everyone had the power to abuse, to hurt others by
their careless actions. He'd also come out of it with a different perspective on the past. He knew now that he'd had
a bad D.I. in the army. The brutality had been in the man,
not in the system of training....

Some time later, still lost in thought, he reached for the
cup of coffee he'd picked up on his way in, took a swallow
and grimaced. "Cold as muddy water," he muttered,
glancing at his watch. He had office hours in fifteen minutes, but he doubted he'd make it through the afternoon
without a caffeine fix. What the hell, he thought, swinging
his feet off the desk, I'm not expecting anyone today anyway.

While Ty was off getting himself another cup of coffee,
Kate was in her kitchen drinking Irish moss tea and impatiently leafing through her business law textbook. She hoped
the herbal brew would have a calming effect on frustration

d indignation, because she had both. As far as she was
oncerned, a contract had been breached.

Ty Raphaell had made no attempt whatsoever to contact
er after all his pontificating on "trusting your fellow man
d good faith negotiations"—and with the next class
oming on the horizon, Kate knew one thing for sure: she
asn't going to sit through another lecture and let him se-
ce her with legalese!

She also knew from the course outline that he held office
ours twice a week from two to four, and that today was one
the designated days. Abruptly, the impulse that had been
uilding in her all week came to a head. "I think a counsel-
g session is in order," she muttered, glancing at her watch.
he slammed her textbook shut. If she left now, she could
ake it with time to spare. She arrived at Ty's office on the
roke of two, found the door hanging open and the law
rofessor in question conspicuously absent. Either he's a
ery busy man or the place has just been ransacked, she de-
ded charitably, noting haphazard stacks of books, news-
apers and reports. More books cluttered his desk, along
ith piles of loose paper and notes. Expecting him to show
at any moment, she entered the wreckage cautiously and
t in the only visitor's chair.

Her impatience turned to uneasiness as the minutes tick-
g away became five and then ten. She'd planned to con-
ont him head-on. *Let's hear it, Professor Raphaell, what's
l this business about Boy Scout oaths, about trusting you
d dancing with you? What did all that mean? Huh, hot-
ot?* That sort of tough talk had sounded pretty good to
er in the car on the way over here, but now that she'd been
elayed, her head of steam was evaporating.

She took the time to reconsider his office, the law books
lling his bookshelves, the tennis racket and cans of balls
ropped in a corner, and finally her scrutiny fell on a
astepaper basket crammed to the brim with something that
oked like research reports. Curious, she slid forward on

the chair, craning to see what they were. She'd read on
word—*Stress*—when a shadow fell over the basket.

"Lose something?"

Kate jerked around and saw her business law professo
looming in the doorway, a cup of coffee in his hand. "No
of course not." She nearly slipped off the chair as she trie
to right herself. "I thought I saw something...on the floor.'

Sighing, she let the doomed excuse die a natural death
She'd always been a lousy liar, and his silent observatio
told her he wasn't buying a word of it anyway. As he walke
to his desk and sat down, an ironic tilt to his mouth, Kat
felt her head of steam returning.

He took a sip of coffee, all very casual, put the cup down
settled back in his chair and propped his foot against th
edge of the desk. "A man's wastebasket is a very privat
thing," he said at last.

"Apparently so." The edge in her voice was intentiona
"But glancing into one is not on a level with stealing fro
the needy, which is how you're making it sound."

"Oh, I don't know," he countered quietly. "How woul
you like me to go through *your* wastebasket?"

Heat warmed her ears. "I...wouldn't." And she didn'
appreciate the object lesson, either.

They stared at each other, stalemated.

Kate felt the warmth spreading down her throat. She'
come here to confront him, and he was chiding her abou
wastebaskets? Unwilling to look away as their standof
continued, she found herself examining his features, relu
tantly aware of his classic bones, his carelessly combed dar
hair and the amused sparks in his eyes. Amused sparks
He'd been kidding her, of course.

She settled back, relaxing her defenses a little.

A millisecond later, without warning, Ty's gaze drifted t
her mouth, and suddenly, *that quickly*, the energy connec
ing them turned electric. Kate's pulse rate nearly went of
the charts.

Caught by the abruptness of it, she crossed her legs and
brought a hand to her throat. Sensations swirled through her
crested state of awareness. Everything seemed to be rushing—her heart, her thoughts, even her eyelids. Her mind
run frantically, searching for something to say. She knew
they'd been talking about something—garbage cans?—but
she couldn't imagine why.

All she could think about, for some ridiculous reason,
was that terribly sad moment weeks ago when she'd given
him his O.R. award. He'd looked heartbreakingly handsome in his uniform, and his smile had been so grave. *It's
been a privilege, Sarge.*

"Kate?"

She blinked and the man across the desk came back into
focus. "So... what have you been doing since graduation?" she asked.

"Teaching, mostly."

"Teaching, *of course.*" It came back to her then. They'd
been talking about his *wastebasket.* "Listen," she said, still
feeling a little short of breath, "you may have a point about
the privacy thing. I probably shouldn't have been...
eyeballing your garbage."

"Ah, the hell with privacy." His voice was husky with
laughter, and his eyes were so vibrant they seemed to shimmer. "Anything I have is yours, Sarge. Including my garbage." He waved a hand toward the basket. "Help yourself."

Irony softened her smile as she glanced at the brimming
basket. "Thanks, that'll tide me over until my next trip to
the dump."

Ty laughed and tipped his coffee cup to her, conceding the
battle. Settling back again, he took a swallow, his offhand-
edness belying the slow, piercing interest in his gaze. "If it
isn't the secrets of my garbage can you're after, then what
brings you here?"

Kate stared at him a moment. The questions she'
planned to confront him with had fallen right out of h
head—along with everything else.

"I guess that was a stumper?" he said, laughing softl
rescuing her. "Never mind. I've got a better question. Wh
are you taking my business law class?"

She shrugged a shoulder, suddenly feeling a little awl
ward about revealing her plans. "I had this crazy idea abou
becoming a detective."

"A *detective*? Kate Madigan, the original Screamin' Blu
Meanie?" He released an intrigued chuckle. "What brough
that on? Hold it," he said, dropping his foot to the floc
and sitting forward. "This sounds like one of those tall
that calls for beaches and sea gulls. What do you say to
walk on the pier?"

"The pier?" Kate wet her lips with a quick, nervous touc
of her tongue. "You remember what happened the last tim
we went to the pier?"

Smiling faintly, Ty scribbled a note on a piece of pape
and walked past her to place it on the door. "That's why
suggested it."

As it turned out, Kate couldn't bring herself to wait fe
their destination to tell him about how she'd changed h
life. Their conversation en route to the pier moved rapidl
through the details of her recent decisions, including h
realization that she'd become a D.I. to silence her gui
about Glenn's accident. Ty acknowledged her progress wit
a nod and three words, "You're amazing, Sarge."

They exchanged glances then, and as he took hold of h
hand, warming it for a moment, the brief meeting of the
eyes spiked to one of those mesmerizing split seconds whe
a man and woman know everything there is to know abou
each other. It stunned them both into silence. Whatever els
they said from that point on was the hushed, fitful talk c
two people who have just been given a naked glimpse of th

ower they have over each other—to bring joy, to love, to
urt.

Finally they were both quiet, silence enveloping them.
Warm and alive, it seemed almost to glow with their awareness of each other. During the last moments of the short
drive, they drew inward, both lost in their own reveries. Kate
was remembering, reliving their prior interlude on the twi-
light beach, the accidental glances, the fleeting contact of
their bodies.

Ty was anticipating, imagining the sweet agony of
touching her again, holding her, claiming her. A familiar
scenario replayed, not so much in his mind as in the nerve
centers of his body and along the periphery of his senses. It
was a dark fantasy of the stormy woman next to him shud-
dering, clinging to him, *needing* him. God, he wanted that.
The thought sparked an impulse in his muscles, and he
tightened his hands on the wheel.

An instant later he slowed the sports car and pulled it over
onto the shoulder of the busy highway. "The pier can wait,"
he said, turning to Kate. "I can't. I want to *dance* with
you."

"Dance?" Her voice had a soft, startled quality.

"We have a binding contract."

"Actually, we don't," she countered, tilting a smile at
him. "Your students were right. The law doesn't recognize
social transactions. I could give you chapter and verse from
the textbook."

"Humor me," he warned, taking her curled hand, kissing the knuckles. "I'm the law professor." He looked up at
her and felt the pulse in her wrist become erratic beneath his
fingers.

Her smile wavered. "Let's dance, Prof."

As he pulled the car back into the stream of traffic, she
touched his arm and said, "My place."

"Are you sure?"

The answer was in her eyes. The slate-gray color held
flashes of silver. Desire was stirring in her gaze and another
beautiful, glittery message he'd seen before…longing. It was
so riveting he had to look away. And even when he did, he
could still feel the brilliance. It was like staring out to sea
and watching the sun shower the water with a thousand
sparkling points of excitement. Am I ready for this? he
wondered. Am I ready to lose my heart and soul to this
woman?

Again, their short trip was made in near silence. There
didn't seem to be any words that could compete with the
aura of expectancy in the car. A charge hung in the air
around them, drawing energy from their excitement and
spilling it over them in a shimmering mist.

Without warning, Ty took her hand, kissed it and laid it
on his thigh, holding it there with his own hand for a moment. The shock of sensation was too much for Kate, and
she pulled back involuntarily, a frisson of heat tingling
through her palm and up her arm. A moment later she
reached out irresistibly and touched him there again, laying
her hand lightly on his leg, feeling his muscles flex under her
touch. By the time they reached her apartment, she was
weak with needing him.

She turned to him the moment they entered the living
room and impulsively touched him again, his face this time.
She grazed the high arc of his cheekbones with her fingertips and then, as she traced the sensual half smile on his lips,
he took her finger into his mouth and suckled it, gently,
erotically.

A painful thrill ripped through Kate's body. This man was
going to kill her softly, she knew that. She would die from
pleasure.

As she drew back, he caught hold of her hand and kissed
each of her fingertips, bathing them with his warm breath.
Staring into her eyes, his features transformed with riveting
intensity. Suddenly his expression was suffused with a ten-

derness she'd never seen before. His cheek muscles flexed and his breath raced in his throat, strong and resonant. "Have I told you that I'm in love with you...irrevocably?"

Kate stared at him, stunned, sure she hadn't heard him right. *"Irrevocably?"*

"Yeah, that's lawyer talk for forever and ever."

"In love?"

He nodded and touched her lips, his fingers trembling a little. "Forever and ever... *I love you*, Sarge."

Kate blinked rapidly and suddenly her eyes were misting, burning with tears. She hadn't realized how badly she wanted to hear those words until he'd said them. The sweet, fiery love in his eyes, the tenderness in his voice made her feel as though her heart would break. "What took you so long, Raphaell?" she said, each word an aching whisper.

Breathing raggedly, he cupped her chin with his hand and tilted her face up to his. "I'm a slow starter, but stick with me," he promised, "I make up for it down the line."

She touched his face again, her hands unsteady as she rose on tiptoes, pressing herself softly to him, cherishing his mouth with hers. All she wanted in the world was to kiss him, hold him...but he broke away from her gently.

"Sarge—" he stroked her face "—there's something else. Do you remember the night I promised to tell you why I really took the training?"

Kate nodded, vaguely uneasy.

"Well it had to do with my days in the army—and the fact that I didn't like drill instructors a hell of a lot." He hesitated, tracing the delicate line of her jaw with his thumb. "I guarantee you, I did *not* expect to fall in love with one. Someday I'll explain what that means, but not tonight."

Staring up at him, her heart brimming over, Kate realized that she hadn't a clue what he was talking about...and it didn't matter. An aching warmth filled her throat. It didn't matter at all. She'd thought she would never love anyone again, but she loved this man so much, blindly. She tried to smile, but her lower lip was too unsteady. "Just a long as you didn't fix that dart game, Raphaell. *That* I could never forgive you for."

He laughed out loud and wrapped her in his arms, nearly hugging the breath out of her. Kate arched back to look up at him, and he bent to kiss her, quickly, breathlessly. His mouth was searingly soft against hers, and cool at first, cool as satin. She sighed with rapturous pleasure as their bodies melted together, the softness of her flesh yielding to the hardness of his.

As the kiss deepened, he penetrated her parted lips with his tongue and Kate felt a sweet rip tide of sensation rising inside her. She moaned softly, tightening against feeling that were glorious and painful. "Make love to me, Ty," she pleaded. "I can't wait any longer."

He swung her into his arms and carried her into the bedroom, depositing her on a cloud bank of ruffled pillows. Lying beside her, pulling her into his arms, he kissed her with consuming passion and then suddenly, hesitating in the heat of it all, he murmured against her lips, "I think we have another slight problem here, Sarge."

"What?" she breathed. "What's wrong?"

He pulled back, searched her eyes. "You're my student. The college frowns on fraternization."

She stared at him, astonished laughter bubbling. Was he kidding? She had no idea, but there did seem to be a glint of something irrepressible in his eyes.

"I think I may know a way around that problem," she said, smiling at him as she unfastened the top button of his shirt. Ignoring his questions, she worked her way down, parting the soft cotton material and tantalizing his collarbone with her lips, her tongue.

"What? You're quitting school?" he gasped, as she slipped her fingers inside his waistband to unsnap his jeans. "*I'm* quitting school?"

"Neither of us is quitting school," she promised him softly, innocently, meeting his gaze as she took indecent liberties with his zipper. "But by the time I'm done with you, Ty Raphaell, I may have to marry you and make an honest law professor out of you."

*   *   *   *   *

1989
IS THE YEAR
OF THE MAN!

What makes a romance? A special man, of course, and Silhouette Desire celebrates that fact with *twelve* of them! From Mr. January to Mr. December, every month spotlights the Silhouette Desire hero—our **MAN OF THE MONTH.**

Sexy, macho, charming, irritating…irresistible! Nothing can stop these men from sweeping you away. Created by some of your favorite authors, each man is custom-made for pleasure—*reading* pleasure—so don't miss a single one.

Diana Palmer kicks off the new year, and you can look forward to magnificent men from **Joan Hohl, Jennifer Greene** and many, many more. So get out there and find your man!

Silhouette Desire's

MAN OF THE MONTH…

MAND-1